# Phantasms in
# the Infirmary

# Phantasms in the Infirmary


# By

# Ram & Julie Gulrajani

# Phantasms
## in the infirmary

a collection of
**ghostly** short stories
and **ghoulish** encounters

by Ram & Julie Gulrajani

*"Now I know what a ghost is.*

*Unfinished business that's what it is."*

Salman Rushdie, The Satanic Verses

# Phantasms in the Infirmary

## A collection of hospital related ghost stories and apparitions.

### Copyright © 2014 RP & JF Gulrajani

7

# Prologue

So you like to be scared?

You must do, otherwise you wouldn't have bought this book... well I hope to not disappoint you with the following collection of ghostly and ghoulish stories.

It is no lie that whilst writing this, it actually frightened me, making me turn and look around the room to check that I had not just seen something that shouldn't have been there such as an uninvited ghostly presence. By this, I did not mean leaving my coffee mug clearly out of place on the dining room table; I meant I started to believe I had felt something sinister or supernatural. I must admit, I got a little freaked out at times and questioned whether I should be writing this or was it wrong and would therefore need to stop the project? Especially as the optimal and inspirational time for me to write was late into the night, dragging on to the early wee hours... including the witching hour. It was enough to give me goose bumps.  Needless to say, I persevered.

So why write about ghosts in hospitals?

Well, few buildings and structures exist that can offer us as much hope and wellness as a hospital can.

Agreed, the publicity is not always favourable but on the whole, hospitals, as the name indicates, offer us refuge, hospitality and a place to recover for the sick and injured in our society.

These buildings are indeed constructed as institutions that guarantee the offer of refuge and caring delivered by trained, dedicated and competent staff. Historically, many of these institutions were developed in countless towns and cities across the globe, growing to the centres of science and medicine that they have now developed into but equally, many were not purpose built for this compassionate outcome.

Numerous hospitals as we know them now, had alternative origins and purposes far from the humanistic functions they now advocate. They were either asylums, orphanages, workhouses, convents or monasteries in the past. Many of these were far from good places to be a resident or patient in and ironically, they certainly did not provide asylum.

Conversely, hospitals are also a place of death. It is not uncommon for the dying to be cared for in these monuments of healthcare. They are a place of compassion for the sick and terminally ill in their last days and moments of life.

The majority of people who die are ready to move on to "the other side", embracing death as part of life and accepting its cold and unavoidable call. Sad and upsetting as death can be, it is inevitable and cannot be cheated; death is a part of life and happens to all.

Then there are those that are far from ready to move on to another plane seeking some form of immortality. Those that have "unfinished business", gripes or other reasons for not wanting to pass on, preferring to linger in the world between life and death. Those that are not alive, but then again are not completely deceased.

They linger, hanging on to this mortal coil for their own reasons in whatever way they can, not ready to let go, their affairs left incomplete for whatever the reason may be. Their presence remains, not always a peaceful one at that. It is with no doubt that an architectural structure like a hospital, due to the many fatalities it has housed, is an ideal venue to haunt in a state of purgatory.

The second reason is that I have spent most of my adult life working in hospitals of one sort or another. The third reason: I had not seen a similar book out there...

This is a collection of some of the many stories I have heard and accumulated over the many decades of practice I have had in healthcare in many of these buildings, some scarier than others. Whether it was the creepy creak of a door, the smell of decay masked by heavy disinfectant, strange noises, glimpses of shadows or selective changes in temperature, they all added to the experience.

Some of these stories have been shared between colleagues in the quiet coffee breaks on busy night shifts, when the witching hour sets itself firmly in on the wards and departments of these eerie edifices. When the nights become dark, cold and creepy, the nurses begin to imagine things and exchange horror stories and ghostly tales.

They retell accounts of these noises that have no source, shadows that have no form, smells that are unfamiliar or unrelated to the environments, things that suddenly move or go missing and the many things going bump in the night.

These stories thankfully did not all happen in one hospital. Can you imagine trying to recruit staff into a haunted hospital? The interview process would certainly include questions like 'what would you do if a ghost appears on your ward?' and 'how far would you run...?'

For the sake of poetic justice, all the stories have been adapted to occur in this one imaginary hospital in one geographical area spanning a good few years. This could be any hospital, anywhere in any country in the world.

Again, for the sake of freedom of expression in the process of exercising this work of fiction, many of the stories are anchored in tales told in many wards. The shared tales have made their way to local folklore and retold by many nurses and doctors who have experienced these inexplicable encounters with ghosts and ghouls in numerous hospital wards, departments and hospitals across the globe.

These stories have happened. They have been recounted to me or my colleagues over the years and now I feel it is my duty to share and scare you with them.

Not all the haunting and apparitions in these monumental buildings are evil. Some are have been considered to be helpful and a good omen. However, come the crunch, I doubt many of us would  look forward to in meeting a spectral force or haunting,

however good they were!

The collected works of contemporary hospital folklore in

this book hopes to demonstrate this.

In reassurance:
It is with true love as it is with ghosts; everyone talks
about it, but few have seen it.
--Francois LaRochefoucauld


Please enjoy this compilation of short stories, however,

be weary of the next time you hear the patient call bell,

it may not always be what you expected.

They are stories after all, or are they?

 Read on if you dare...

## St Augustus Hospital

As the population grew in the surrounding city, the infrastructure supporting it had to expand with it.

Not only did the practical daily facilities such as the Electricity and water supplies, sewers, schools and policing needed to be added to it but more important services were also required to develop.

This expansion also included transport resources, shopping facilities and of course the local hospital. The laws of supply and demand applied to healthcare too.

No large metropolis is complete without adequate healthcare facilities. All these essential public services needed to expand and grow in order to absorb the added demands, extra workload and needs of the additional citizens and service users.

The old tuberculosis sanatorium, St Augustus, had been a Victorian workhouse in days gone by. Before that it had been a convent for a holy order of nuns and an old psychiatric unit or lunatic asylum as they were commonly referred to. The building had stood there, commanding its surroundings as it towered out of the fields since the early 1800's. It was constructed for functionality and not beauty with its primary purpose, to house the workforce, the poor, unwell, the mentally ill and the dying. It allowed the further expansion of the settlement, permitting the more wealthy and salubrious creations in the town through its success as a workhouse.

Its vast ramparts, like a gigantic fortification, could be seen for miles and as it expanded, it had become even more visible in the local panorama, eroding into the vast undulating grounds that enveloped this structure.

The erected building oozed strength and power through its functional architecture. It was both an iconic and ironic proof of affluence.

St Augustus was bordered by a small wooded area with tall oak and silver birch trees whose branches spread out as if trying to cover additional area. The undulating emerald green pastures was slashed by a blue flowing brook that cut through its otherwise faultless and picturesque landscape and towered into the skyline. The Gothic construction itself was aligned by Greek style columns and large windows that allowed the passage of light into the large rooms and halls secreted within it. The light that bounced in the building revealed an

architectural structure that was not solid but one
peppered with corridors that led further into a
multitude of rooms with high ceilings supported by
elaborately constructed pillars and large plastered walls.
Like a vast bee hive, its halls and corridors led endlessly
to other passages and quarters. The beams of bright
light that entered this construction through its arch
shaped windows also painted a plethora of shapes and
shadows on the stark walls that were occasionally
embellished by large paintings. These ornately framed
but stark paintings, mostly portraits, representations of
the medics and matrons who had commanded its many
corridors, sauntered through its wards and made St
Augustus what it was.

Among these were also the portraits of high powered
benefactors that had contributed to the buildings
maintenance and expansion. Painted by relatively
famous artists and encased in flamboyant frames to
promote their generosity to the community using the
edifice. This overt showcasing of community spirit and

generosity was an outward act of charity and a badge of honour.  A small return for their financial backing: A small area of wall within the inner sanctum of the construction to hang from for relative eternity. The main structure was surrounded by a multitude of out-buildings, extensions and appendages to the main construction that had slowly eaten into the acres of fields that surrounded the original workhouse.

The workhouse had taken in orphans and children whose unmarried mothers had entrusted them into the care of the institution. The directors of these places worked its occupants with long hours, poor work conditions and dangerous surroundings. They also took in some of these unmarried young mothers themselves. They had usually been forced into the workhouse by their shamed parents during the prudish Victorian era, an age where the dishonour and humiliation of having a child out of wedlock, a bastard, was worse than never seeing their baby ever again. The workhouse also took in the gutter snipes, rug-rats, waifs and strays that

21

roamed the dark and cold streets, slept in alleyways, stealing and robbing to make amends in order to survive and stay alive. Their schooling was the " University of life or the school of hard knocks". There was no formal education being offered and keeping hunger at bay was these children's priority. The expertise they acquired by manning the many looms, machines and mechanical monsters that the industrial revolution created. Their dexterity and small limbs being a feature of their use, however risky this may have been. This ensured that their skills in crime could be stemmed if they were taken in to the workhouse. These children were made to work in the dangerous intricate machinery. The infinite supply of small hands that the age offered coupled with a lack of health and safety made this a very dangerous but profitable building. Unfortunately, the profits were more important.

 These little urchins could manage the technology and its moving parts better than the cumbersome hand of an adult... This was far from being charitable. It was business!

The children of the workhouses and poorly paid labour helped the productivity and expansion of the area. In the interim, it made the area safer and more marketable to other industries therefore perpetuating the establishment's growth and in turn, requiring more cheap labour, a vicious cycle of supply and demand.

Many of the children would eventually leave the workhouse, either by being employed by other factories or by working in the ship building docks that moved into the area during the industrial revolution.

Some never left...

They would form part of the mythology and history of the place. They were the unfortunate ones that were either killed by industrial accidents, diseases caused by the unsanitary conditions they lived in, malnutrition or other unexplained reasons that no one apparently knew of or cared about. Child abuse was rife at the time as well as corporal punishment. Neglect, sexual abuse, physical torture, mental abuse was commonplace. The poor children were not nurtured, loved or wanted. It was a very different age to ours. Children were castigated for the minimum of misdemeanours. Their punishments included being hit with sticks, belts and even kicked at times.

They would be starved and imprisoned for days on end in dank dark rooms, cells by any other name or description. Some would lose their lives through these infringements and inhuman cruelty and no one seemed to be bothered by this. There seemed to be boundless resources, many more street kids and orphans to replace the dead ones!

The ones that left the building alive would attempt to lead relatively productive and meaningful lives but would forever be tortured by the scars of their experiences and unpleasant memories. Their efforts were driven by the need to endeavour to avoid these institutions for the rest of their lives.

The ones that never left were buried in the grounds small and shamefully undignified cemetery. Pauper's graves did not register a name, age or memory. The only remembrance or proof of their existence was the meticulously maintained register the workhouse superintendent kept. A record of the child's name, age, short description of their work title, admission date plus "disposal date and method", a harsh but descriptive discharge date documenting the manner of removal from the premises, dead or alive...

After the abolition of the workhouses and the demise of the industrial revolution, St Augustus became the "lunatic asylum" or "Mad House". It was then that the first big extension was added to the original structure. It was created in order to accommodate those with mental illness but others also resided within. Additional wards had been created, dedicated to the popular diagnoses of the age: schizophrenic's, hypo-manics, sociopaths, psychopaths, depressives and people with learning disabilities. Many of the long term inpatients were children of the workhouse. They had grown up into institutionalised adults, dependent on the routines and structured rules of St Augusts, unable to leave. They found that they were unable to function on their own in society. They were destined to stay within the confines of these walls. The hospital inmates also included those who displayed an interest in the same sex.

Homosexuality was seen as a mental disease and the supposedly eminent minds of the time had decreed that they needed to be kept away from others in society to stop the infection onto "normal people". They endured horrific treatments and experiments such as aversion therapies, electrical shock therapy and beatings, lots of beatings. These were based on little or no research and generally resulted in more harm than benefit.

Conditions were far from ideal; the unit had a ratio of sixty patients to a ward, crammed in a space where now, twenty would fit comfortably.

A strong room and two padded cells were built to allow staff to restrain and incarcerate those in crisis before the advent of medications such as anti-psychotic drugs that chemically control and assist patients now.

A further two wards were constructed to house another type of patient with the epidemic of sexually transmitted diseases that existed. There were a large number of patients suffering from General Paralysis of the Insane (GPI). This was a tertiary result of syphilis that was rife in that era. It was caused through the high prostitution rates that existed in the pre-penicillin era. Its treatments at the time included shoving hot pokers in the genital area to try and burn out the infection, religious intervention and herbal lotions and potions that were anything but effective. The consequences of this was the infection developed until the nervous

27

system was involved causing the manifestation of tertiary syphilis and its madness.

Unprotected sex with a street whore or one of the many houses of ill repute that sprouted around the industrial areas of the emerging city was easy for the increasing workforce. The lack of obvious moral fibre, poor financial security and lack of skills sadly made prostitution an easy trade to fall into.

Tertiary syphilis and its materialization were scary. A distinctive shuffling gait, hallucinations and psychotic behaviours with mood swings, collapse and incomprehensible conversations and ramblings were among the many manifestations of the worsening disease.

The asylum for the insane was far from clinically conducive to recovery. The screams and shouts, odd behaviours and smells were a hindrance to recovery. The staff which consisted mainly of a battalion of male orderly's, ex-service men, soldiers and sailors. They had left their respective service, many scarred by their experiences in battle and who were built like boxers. They were strong and solid, many with a low I.Q. who had little or no formal nurse training. They had few other skills but were useful in fights, restraining and protecting the pioneering psychiatrists and occasional untrained nurses who were mostly well meaning gentry.

In those days there were   few if any patient rights or charters, deprivation of liberty was rife.

The prescribed treatments were far from sophisticated and quite barbaric. Electroconvulsive Therapy (ECT) and sleep treatments were frequently used as were aversion therapies and a lot of restraining. Restraint was not limited to tying patients to beds and chairs; it included padded cells where seclusion in a padded and claustrophobic room prevented the staff from getting harmed and stopped the patient from hurting themselves. It was tantamount to cruel imprisonment added to which the use of a strait jacket to boot seemed to be the orders of the day.

Patients hated this more than anything else and they would fight and scream, bite and kick in order to free themselves however rarely succeeding in avoiding this punishment.

Thankfully, science helped evolve the hospital into a model more in-keeping with what we know now and expect. It soon filled up with doctors and trained nurses, order and reduction in cross infection, medicaments and antibiotics, accident and emergency departments with up to the minute research and evidence based therapies with the patient at the centre of treatment.

 Healing and recovery outweighed death and disease as the main outcomes. For the terminally ill, a dignified death with their loved ones at and was expected. The built environment was transformed, St Augustus had evolved into a temple of healing; however the scars of its past could not be forgotten, in one way they refused to be ancient history by the sightings, sounds and apparitions that were frequently reported and spoken about.

## <u>The Visiting Angel</u>

Throughout St Augustus' life, existence and being, there had been numerous rumours of ghostly apparitions, strange lights, unearthly sounds and noises, piercing screams from beyond the grave and bizarre shadows in the many rooms, wards and corridors that were secreted within the old building.

That feeling of "not being alone", that there was "something else" there with you was ever present. The building felt haunted and many of its live inhabitants shared the negative and unnerving feeling.

There were copious stories of objects moving on their own, propelling themselves across surfaces lacking any logical explanation.

There were tales of poltergeist activity aplenty, ghostly movers and shakers at their clinical best, or at their worst. It was dependent on the views of the witnesses. Local legends and numerous shared stories of bits and pieces of equipment, patient's personal belongings and even food going missing. Some of the recollections told of things suddenly disappearing for no obvious reasons or explanation in front of witnesses eyes. People had recounted and experienced unearthly and unexplainable creepy noises, squeaky floors and footsteps that had no apparent or visible physical source. This was not all. There were sudden

34

temperature changes, not in keeping with the weather and were isolated to certain areas of high spectral activity. Chillingly cold environments which were suddenly experienced by staff or patients, coming and going within minutes, like a passing visitation from another plane or world.

Then there were the smells... an assault to the olfactory system. It was the combined smell of rotting flesh and sulphur some described as "rotten eggs" by witnesses to these unearthly events.

The incidents were sporadic. There were no patterns associated with lunar cycles, thunderstorms or seasons. There was nothing that could give an alternative or logical reason for these events and spine-chilling occurrences. They were however freaky and disturbing for those experiencing them with many feeling quite ill soon after these events. However, there were links with certain patients on wards who had been admitted with certain diagnoses.

Ward 7 was a prime example of the demonic demonstrations that could be experienced in this edifice. This was the female surgical ward in which patients were admitted to undergo general surgical operations and procedures but in the main, it was a ward that housed patients undergoing gynaecological operations, including oncology. Cancer patients would be admitted to receive gynaecological treatments and invasive interventions. They would be admitted for treatment, observation, monitoring and surgery so it was quite a busy ward.

The apparitions in ward 7 seemed to be directly linked to patients admitted with cervical cancer. The ghost was described as 'a friendly ghost' or 'an angel' who would manifest itself on the ward, appearing beside the patient with that specific malignant diagnosis, especially if they were in the terminal phase of their illness.

There had been several sightings and reports of the spectral force over the many years and no matter how friendly the ghost was reported to be, it was still unnatural and unexpectedly disturbing.

It was on one specific night shift on ward 7 during a clement and warm summers evening that student nurse Joleyne Forde had been allocated to work and experience the night time care of the surgical patients as part of her nurse training that she encountered this soul.

The shift had started at 8pm and would last until the next morning, 12 hours later. A 12 hour shift that would stretch through the early hours and complete at 8am the next morning. It took a lot of resolve and energy to cope with the demands on both body and mind in order to maintain a caring sharpness through the night.

Although she had worked on ward 7 for a few weeks, she had only worked the day shifts; this was her inaugural night shift, the first of three.

The ward routine included monitoring temperatures, blood pressures, pulses and respiratory rates, balancing the many fluid balance charts that should include the fluids taken orally or intravenously as well as the bodily fluids expelled. This included urine, vomit and any haemorrhaging.

Drains, catheter bags and bedpans were also emptied with meticulous charting for the 30 patients on the ward as the comfort rounds were continued. These patients were also given a night time drink and made comfortable, pain relieving drugs issued as well as any night sedation or routine medications administered in the last drug round of the day.

The ward was staffed by three members of staff, 2 qualified and 1 unqualified members of staff. Joleyne was not counted in the numbers as students were supernumerary however this specific night, one member of staff had reported sick so the ratio was down but this team were resilient, flexible and would manage.

Tea breaks and meal breaks were organised by the senior member of staff and were planned from 12 midnight onwards. There were always two members of staff on duty on the ward at one time with the senior nurse close by in case there was an emergency to be dealt with.

All the jobs had to be completed before 10pm as this was lights out time. The ward would then transform from a bright clinical setting to a dark and eerily quiet corridor, the silence only being broken by the sound of wind emanating from patients back sides as they snored and farted their way through the night!

The large ward was lit tastefully by sporadic night lights at occasional intervals, enough to distinguish things but without being able to see too much detail. The nurses relied on their trusted torches, an essential piece of kit to discharge ones many differing tasks in the darkness of the night shift. Without the extra light from their pocket torches, the details of temperature and blood pressure readings would be nothing than a blur, incomprehensible and of no value.

There were no admissions planned from the Accident and Emergency department. The ward was quiet with only twenty two beds occupied and there were no issues or problems to report.  The routine tasks were finished and the night had transcended into the early hours without event or incident.

Joleyne had been on her meal break and had returned to the ward. She was now sitting at the nurses' station busily reading her surgical nursing text books and catching up with her studies. Staff nurse Maggie Jones had now left the ward to go for her meal break. Emma the unqualified member of staff was making them a well-earned cup of coffee in the ward kitchen. It was now all pleasantly and serenely quiet.

Suddenly, the silence was disturbed by a loud "Buzz", startling Joleyne, the nurse call buzzer had gone off and the young nursing student looked over at the board that indicated that the light on bed three in bay three was the culprit. The patient on this bed obviously needed her help and assistance.

She stood up and looked at her handover sheet, a piece of paper she had written some notes on about the patients, in order to get more of an idea of who was who and what they needed. She quickly established that it was occupied by Chloe Stark.

Mrs Stark had advanced cervical cancer and at only forty eight years of age, was quite young to be at this palliative stage of the disease. There was no cure and the aim of treatment was to control symptoms in order to keep Mrs Stark as comfortable as possible until the end of life which was now not as distant as her age would dictate.

She was not on any strong pain relieving drugs such as morphine or any other opioids however she was quickly climbing The World Health Organisation's pain ladder, a guide to the escalation and up-titration of pain relieving drugs. She had been admitted to the ward due to heavy bleeding from her vagina and needed to undergo a planned procedure the next day to  stem the cancerous haemorrhage..

Joleyne now put her blue cardigan over her shoulders to stem the night time chill and made her way to the bay three.

The entrance to the ward was now behind her as she walked purposefully toward her patient in need. The dimly lit ward ahead of her cast some strange shadows but she marched on. Focused, torch in hand, in case she required extra illumination and eyes peeled, ears tuned in to anything sinister or unusual bounded down the old corridor.

She walked closer to the bay and noticed that all else seemed quiet and there was nothing else to action other than to assist Mrs. Stark. Once she arrived at the four bedded bay,  she noticed that the patient was sitting up in bed, looking comfortable and the bed seemed to have been tidied up as nurses tend to do in order to make the patient look less untidy and the bed space less cluttered. The call buzzer light was still flashing so Joleyne turned this off as she lightly held Mrs Stark's hand and addressed her.

'Are you okay Mrs. Stark?' she enquired 'is there anything I can help you with?'

Mrs Stark smiled and replied 'sorry for calling you nurse, I know you are busy but I was bleeding heavily from "down below" and so wanted a new pad however I also required some help in changing it as I feel a little weak'.

'Well of course' Joleyne retorted 'I will go and get you a pad and will be back in a moment to help you with it'

Mrs Stark then said something quite surreal 'no its okay dear, the other nurse has already helped me with it, she was very efficient, gentle and kind but very quiet, it must be from working nights for so long eh?' She quipped.

'Oh, I thought Emma was in the kitchen making us some coffee, she could have turned the buzzer off then' Joleyne replied politely.

'No, not Emma, that lady there wearing the white uniform and hat' the patient replied as she pointed towards the corridor.

The young student turned around to face the dark corridor, puzzled by the patient's description of the nurse, especially as no nurses in the hospital wore white uniforms. Furthermore, hats had not been worn by nurses in decades. It was then that her questions were answered as she saw the nurse that had assisted her patients call for help. Joleyne was now facing a very pale looking figure, almost translucent in her white uniform and white hat in situ looking back at them. A pale face starred at her, a pallor that seemed to glow against the contrasting deep darkness in the background. Although she stood only a few feet away she could not recognise this nurse.  It certainly wasn't Emma or Maggie.

The fledgling nurse immediately felt goose-bumps across her body; the hairs on the back of her neck were standing to attention as her pulse rate rose and blood pressure dropped. She felt faint and queasy as she stared at the figure across from her. She was transfixed but could feel her legs start to quickly go weak beneath her although she had to remain standing, not only to not frighten the patient but also in case she needed to run.

As she stood there, she was still holding on to Mrs. Stark's hand, unintentionally squeezing her hand with her now excessively sweaty palms as she gripped tight in fear.

'Are you okay Joleyne?' the patient asked in an ironic reversal of roles.

'Erm ... I, I, I think so?' she muttered back.

'You're shivering and gripping my hand so tightly, are you sure you are alright?' she probed.

At that moment and before she could muster a reply, with her focus on the apparition that was unaccounted and absent from the staff roster, she noticed a smile emanate from this ghostly phantom as she disappeared into the darkness. She did not move away, she had just disintegrated into the darkness, vanished.

'Yes, sorry Mrs. Stark, yes, I am fine, thank you, sorry' she now replied slowly coming back to her senses. 'I am glad you are okay, please get some rest and try to sleep, you have a busy day ahead of you tomorrow, call us if you need any further help'

Joleyne now tucked the patient in, made her comfortable and hurried down the corridor in search of solace, comfort and maybe some explanation from her colleagues. She looked back down the corridor several times to check for any other unexplained beings but there was no one else there.

As she approached the nurses' station, Emma was turning out of the kitchen and Joleyne jumped out of her skin as she gave out a high pitched screech.

Emma nearly dropped the small tray with the two hot drinks and a plate full of biscuits elegantly arranged on it.

'Whoa, what in heaven's name is wrong, you nearly made me spill the bloody drinks with your jumpiness?' Emma asked the young nurse. 'Are you okay Joleyne, you look spooked, like you have just seen a ghost?'

'I don't know' she replied, 'I may have done, I'm not sure...'

'Tell me what you have seen Joleyne' asked Emma.

'I'm not sure what I have just seen, well I can't explain it anyway' Joleyne replied, her voice now shaky and her tone, low. With her voice still trembling and goose-bumps the size of hives, she took her cardigan off in automatic pilot mode with an expressionless face and sat heavily on a chair at the desk. The young student nurse was handed her warm beverage by her colleague and grasped it with both hands, tightly but still with a noticeable shake that caused some of the hot coffee to spill.

Joleyne now started to recount the recent and mysterious events that had occurred in bay 3. Explaining how she had got to the lady with the cervical cancer at her request and by the time she got there, she had already been assisted by someone else 'something like a ghost or spectre 'she added.

Emma smiled and said 'its okay Joleyne, someone should have told you about Grace'.

'Grace who?' She replied, confused by the statement.

'Grace used to be a nurse in this hospital in the 1960's. Grace tragically died on this ward in 1965, from cervical cancer' Emma explained.

Joleyne was now even more confused and additionally frightened having had her suspicions confirmed that what she had encountered was in fact a ghost. This was not something she was comfortable with, after all it was unusual and freaky to say the very least, not what she had signed up to be a nurse for. She had certainly not covered ghostly apparitions in any of her learning modules in university. She sat in stony silence, listening on to her colleague as she added more to the mystery.

'Grace died from her disease and since then, any patient admitted with the same diagnosis gets a visit from Grace' 'She is very helpful, reassuring, compassionate and does no harm, none of the patients ever get freaked out by her, it's just us nurses that get scared by her appearance but that is only on the first few meetings' Emma explained with an almost casual manner.

'Do you mean I may see her again?' Joleyne stuttered with a less than eager tone to her voice.

Emma continued 'Grace has been known appear to patients on the ward, to counsel them and comfort them, explain to them about cancer, how to accept their fate, relax and reassure them by lifting their spirits, pardon the pun, where no one else could, reducing their anxiety and pain'.

These were all positives to sharing a shift with an apparition but it was difficult to accept for the novice nurse who had only just had her first encounter with a phantasm.

At this point, Maggie returned from her break to find Emma counselling the young student nurse.

'Don't tell me' she exclaimed, almost brutishly, 'Grace has been doing her rounds then?' she joked. 'Is this your first meeting with Grace Joleyne?' she asked.

The reply was short and sweet 'Yes'.

'Well don't worry yourself my dear, it could be worse, you could have encountered one of the others...'

Joleyne gulped as she heard those words and hoped she would not meet any other historical members of the hospital staff, no matter how friendly or well intentioned they were.

At least not on this night shift, one ghost was enough for anyone.

## <u>The Key to the Gates of Hell</u>

It was a calm, warm and humid summers evening. The sun was still hanging in the sky, about to capitulate to the moon and darkness. It was swiftly nearing the end of an otherwise run of the mill and mundane evening shift if ever there was a mundane shift in a hospital.

The nurses had been busy managing the ward and patients in their charge. The doctors had a fairly easy day and the juniors had coped well with the demands on their developing skills.  There had been no peculiarly difficult or complex issues to deal with. All was otherwise well in the old hospital.

There were plenty of available beds for any unplanned emergency admissions, a welcome change from the critical need for empty beds in the hectic winter crisis months.

To add to the perfection of the dying day, there were no staffing issues to address. No sickness or Human resources Issues to deal with, all was great.

8pm: the evening shift were handing over to the night shift who would take on the mantle for the next 12 hours. They would pass on the charge of the patients they'd looked after and rest before taking on their responsibility from them on the next morning, like a massive health related relay race however the metaphorical baton was a ward full of ill people.

A capable and experienced lot, there would be every confidence that the handover the next morning at 8am would be equally as uneventful.

The variety and wide array of tasks to undertake were being assigned to staff with the pressing onslaught of the dark night hours ahead as staff gathered as much information about the patients they would be caring for and looking after on this shift.

The senior nurses on each ward and department were now busy allocating jobs as well as the night time breaks being assigned to their respective nursing teams.

The night manager, Alice was doing her rounds of the whole hospital to check on staff and highlight or resolve any issues before they amounted to irresolvable ones. She visited each ward in turn, spoke to staff and gathered any information she could regarding those patients who were critically ill or dying in order to ensure there were no surprises during the night.

She would meticulously review care plans and supervise the staff to ensure they were equipped with any and all eventualities. All remained well.

As the hours of darkness took hold of the hospital the shadows become longer, the routine work was completed which meant the main lights were turned off. This now meant the nurses would need to be acutely aware of the occurrences of the ward and rely on their other senses in order to achieve complete management of their patients. They would also rely on the range of night lights and torches they possessed to visualise any observations that required looking at.

One by one, in no specific order, the hospital became darker and quieter. As the random lights turned off soon the hospital was steeped in darkness, enveloped by the black curtain of night. The only light that cut through the deep darkness were the dim night lights, very low wattage bulbs that were attached to the main lights that merely glowed, enough to see things without too much definition. There were also randomly placed lamps that shone over the nurse's stations, enough to read with without disturbing the sleeping patients.

The only main lights on were those in the Accident and Emergency department. These remained on in order to invite any patients needing attention and allow a detailed assessment of those requiring treatments.

12:30 am: The rest breaks had started.

These relatively short pauses in work would allow staff an hour of respite and recovery.

The staff on permanent nights, creatures of habit, would always meet up with their friends and colleagues in the hospital canteen on the ground floor. They would always take the first break and have a natter, eat their snacks, share a cigarette or two outside the restaurant until their time to return to work had arrived again.

The next set would then go on their break and so on.

1:45 am: It was just after the clocks had struck a quarter to the hour when the mundane night shift swiftly changed pace to become a night to remember. It would become a shift that would enter the annals of folklore for the wrong reasons.

The first break shift returned to the wards, refreshed and ready to take on the night. Just as the next set of eager staff were about to leave their wards, the strange and sinister occurrences began.

Staff members were unable to leave the wards; the doors were slammed shut and could not be budged, as if these heavy wooden doors had been transformed into locked heavy metal doors that were further weighed down by some powerful invisible force holding them closed. It did not matter who or how hard they tried, the staff could not open the doors. They pushed, budged and heaved with no avail. This was not just happening on one ward but all the wards and departments. Panic stricken, some nurses screamed, some swore and some just stood there, rooted to the spot in confusion.

Within seconds, there were other strange and ghostly unexplained phenomena manifesting themselves.

There were not only things going bump in the night but crashing, screaming, ghoulish laughter  and footsteps that had no obvious source. Closed cupboards opened, linen and equipment flew out and the metal bedpans, receivers and bowls flew off the shelves and clanked on the floor as they crashed to a halt. The taps in the bathrooms and basins turned on as water poured from them, gushing out to add to the cacophony of sound. Lights flickered on and off, giving out an electric buzz as they did so and the ceiling fans spun clockwise, stopped then spun anticlockwise.  A strange smell of rotten flesh could now be detected. It was a strong and pungent unpleasant odour, like a chicken that has just reached its "use by" date as it is taken out of a fridge and the stench hist the nostrils of the poor bugger holding it.

The warm night had now turned frosty and as the panic stricken staff screamed and spoke to each other, they could see the cloudy mists of warm air emanating from their warm bodies. It was very unnatural and unnerving.

'Quick, telephone the night manager' Chloe asked Clarissa on ward 10.

Chloe hastily picked up the phone receiver and listened for the dialling tone before depressing the numbers on the phone pad. She screamed and threw the receiver heavily on the desk as she backed off. Her colour had been drained from her face, she was scared.

'What is wrong Chloe for God's sake, you're worrying me?' Clarissa enquired worriedly.

'It, it's a strange and unearthly voice 'Chloe stammered.

'So what did it say?' she continued.

Her answer was one that made even the most experienced of nurse turn as white as the clinical sheets they used on the beds...

'It said, put that down or die'

'Oh my God, what is going on? Are we going to die?' yelled one of the other staff members who had joined the worried huddle.

'No, no of course not we aren't going to die, don't be silly, it's just someone playing a sick prank, a joke on all of us, give me that phone' Clarissa demanded.

She replaced the receiver on the office phone and proceeded to pick up the receiver and direct it to her ear in search of a dial tone. As if by sheer mimicry, she too slammed the phone on the desk and stepped back away from it. Not a word came from her lips as she now slumped back against the green office wall and snuck out of it, in an attempt to slowly get some distance from this haunted handset, pulling her colleagues out with her as she did, cowering away towards the noisy ward.

Patients were now screaming in the confusion as the din continued with the addition of the incessant buzzing from all the call buzzers joining in the unearthly cacophony that now seemed to fill the previously peaceful night. It was like a demented symphony with no harmony.

The banging, clanking, crying, buzzing and gushing of water now accentuated by unearthly screams as if from beyond the grave. The groaning was echoing as it emanated from behind walls and from inside cupboards. Like a band of crazed banshees, whooping and yelling in order to scare all that may be in earshot. The lights now flickered on and off at an even faster and random rate. The general atmosphere of mayhem and chaos now surreal in its manifestation was like a scene from a "hammer house of horrors" script, all that was missing was the clap of thunder and a caped vampire making an appearance.

Heavy drip stands were moving on their own, as if pushed by someone however, there was no body thrusting them forward. They were quickly stopping at access points in the wards, obstructing the doors further.  The many monitors that were dotted around the wards and departments had now joined in the pandemonium as they picked up heart rates and EEG readings that were not real as the sources of these were pulse less, body less entities.  Intravenous fluid bags were now exploding, releasing their otherwise life sustaining fluids freely onto the surrounding environment. More bedpans fell and crashed on the hard floors. The disharmony that now surrounded the staff and patients was getting unbearable.

The nurses, although scared themselves, tried to reassure the tearful, confused and frightened patients. They fulfilled their function, consoling the patients and putting others before themselves but yet, unable to offer any answers to the multitude of questions fired at them.

'Nurse, what is happening? What is going on?'

'What in heaven's name is going on? 'Why is the whole place going crazy?'

'Nurse, are we being invaded? Is it a war?'

'Nurse, I am frightened, please help me'

They had no answers to the many enquiries and it was worryingly not stopping when suddenly, as quickly as it had started, all the supernatural activity ceased. A stony silence had now replaced the furore that had preceded and for once was welcomed by all.

The wards were dark again. The noises, lights, smells and chaos had been brought to a halt.

The doors were fully functional again, as in the fact that they could be opened easily. The gushing faucets had stopped adding to the now flooded bathrooms, kitchens and hand washing areas.

Nurses and other staff members around the hospital comforted each other, protectively holding patients as patients also held on to each other in reassurance.

1:52 am: Seven minutes of hell on earth had seemed like a great deal longer. They were glad "It" was all over, whatever the cause of this was; it was certainly not a mass hallucination.

The priority was to now return everything back to normal settle people in, clear up and try and get to the route of the issue.

Ward 10's phone was ringing and Chloe and her colleagues looked at each other, hesitant to pick up, fearful of what they would encounter.

They had heard the voices of a demon and did not fancy hearing the evil voice again.

Clarissa as the senior nurse, plucked up the courage and said, I'll do it'.

She trembled as she reached for the receiver on the still ringing telephone. She grabbed it and wearily placed it to her face and spoke softly...

'Hello' she enquired. 'Hello, who is it please?' She continued.

The relief in her face was evident as the colour returned to her pale cheeks, a rosy glow replacing the dusky colour that she and her colleagues had taken on.

'It's okay, it's Aaron from ward 8, asking if we are okay'

'Well I think we are all okay, everyone is a trifle spooked but we are all still alive, I suppose that is okay' she tittered nervously.

Aaron worked in the male medical ward downstairs and was calling to see if anyone needed assistance.

Clarissa continued to chat to her colleague from the other ward... 'we are just clearing up and helping the patients relax and getting them back in their beds, I think we're going to need more Diazepam and that's just for the staff' she joked.

Aaron had offered their services once they had finished their chores and spoken to Alice, the night manager.

'Alice, has anyone spoken to her, is she okay?' Clarissa asked concerned for her safety.

'No I haven't seen her since around 11pm' replied Aaron.

'She would have been on her own in her office, poor love' Clarissa stated.

Although Alice was the senior nurse on nights, she would have been as scared and confused as everyone and anyone else.

At precisely this point, the ward doors slammed open and Alice staggered in. She was pale, sweaty and dazed, as in a state of shock.

'Oh dear Alice, sit down' Chloe insisted as she guided her by the arm to a chair held firmly with the other.

'I'll make you a nice strong cup of tea' added another one of the nurses as she headed toward the kitchen.

'Tea would be more than appreciated, thank you though something stronger would have been better but tea will have to do' Alice acknowledged as she sat on the chair in an attempt to compose herself.

Alice now sat and spoke softly, still shocked and stunned by the recent high jinks. She had just gone for a quick cigarette when all hell broke loose. She had seen and heard everything and was puzzled by what she described as a 'multitude of unearthly forms, shadows and lights' appear out of nowhere and head towards the intensive care unit (I.C.U.).

'Why I.C.U.?' they asked themselves, it was too specific. Their mission now was to establish some facts on what had happened in I.C.U to have attracted all this paranormal attention and activity, ensure the workforce were not harmed and gather any evidence to prevent any further recurrences.

Alice called the I.C.U. on the now safe phone. There was no answer. She tried again and again but to no avail, there was still no reply. 'That is very strange, they aren't busy because they have no patients in the unit' she added bemused and worried.

'I need to get there as soon as possible'. She took a big slurp of tea and added 'who's coming with me, I need at least a couple more volunteers to check on them?'

Clarissa volunteered but with the condition that they were accompanied by a male member of staff. Alice agreed and called ward 8. This time, the call yielded a reply, it was Aaron, the staff nurse who had called earlier.

'Hi, yes its Alice here, I need you to accompany myself and Clarissa to I.C.U. please'. Her assertion was returned with the affirmation that he would and she then hung up, held her cup of tea and sipped it readily with the next 3 gulps emptying the cup. 'Boy did I need that, thanks ladies' she returned.

Within seconds, Aaron rushed in and Alice now looked at Clarissa and said 'right let's get down to business, are you all ready?' she enquired as she lifted herself from the safety and comfort of her chair.

With no further words, the three brave members of the night shift headed to the presumed source of the unearthly activities.

Alice asked a member of staff to call security and ask them to meet them in I.C.U. as they left the ward on their crusade.

They raced through the now dark and relatively quiet corridors and staircases of the old building and finally got to the six bedded unit. They pressed the intercom system and an audible buzz was heard.  After a few seconds wait, there was no answer so Alice called again. Once more there was no reply. They were not going to try again, Alice placed her reading glasses on the bridge of her nose, opened her folder and searched for the entry code to enter into the keypad. Once she had found it, she looked over her spectacles and punched in the numbers in their sequence...' C1469X' she said out loud as she carried out this procedure and then "click" they were in.

Aaron pushed the door open and the intrepid few entered the I.C.U. It was a scene like those described of the Marie Celeste, the legendary ghost ship. The unit was deserted, dark and ghostly. They had entered into what could have been described as a bomb site. There was equipment, papers, beds, books, bowls and other assorted items strewn around the place in no order or purpose, ever There was equipment, papers, beds, books, metal bowls and other assorted items strewn around the place in no order or purpose, everything seemed out of place. The papers that littered the floors were a mix of observation charts, notes and request forms that would need to be sorted but this was not the priority. Luckily there were no patients in the unit, the staff had been kept in the unit as a precaution had they needed to admit someone in. They still needed to find the three nurses on duty and their whereabouts were far from obvious. 'Johnny, Barrie, Dawn where are you?' Alice called out.

There were no answers. Aaron switched on the main lights to aid their exploration. They searched high and low, under piles of equipment and debris, behind doors and in cupboards. There was no sign of any of them... Alice remembered that there was also a third year student on duty with them for the shift and she was also missing.

'Let's try the office' Clarissa said and directed themselves toward it. As they did so, two security men dashed in, red faced and puffed out considering the events of the last half hour and the amount of ground they had covered with the increased work generated. They had certainly earned their money tonight.

'Any one hurt?' asked one of the breathless men.

'We don't know yet' was the reply from Alice as she continued to crouch down and look for the missing members of her team.

All of a sudden, the security man said 'hush, I can hear something'

The search party went very quiet, enough to hear a pin drop and then, they heard the whimpered cry emanating from the isolation room next to the office. They entered the room with caution, like a scene from a police movie, minus the guns and the words "cover me".

Three staff members were lying on the floor, they were unconscious but Barrie was still missing. They then heard a faint cry for help, it was coming from a cupboard in the room. The security staff opened the door and Barrie slumped out, dazed and pallid. He groaned and said, 'help me please, I told them not to do it but they didn't listen to me'.

They helped him out of the confines of the small cupboard and assisted him onto the bed where he slumped again. Clarissa gave him a sip of water, holding his head as she tipped the tumbler containing the life giving fluid.

'Thank you' he replied and his eyes opened further. He then repeated what he had said earlier ' I told them not to do it..' at which point Alice interrupted him 'what do you mean Barrie, not do what?'.

'The Ouija board, I told them it wasn't safe, it wasn't a game, it was dangerous and not clever to play with it but they insisted and...'

Alice interrupted him again 'and all hell broke loose, yes we know'. 'Right, let's get everyone checked out, call a medic and make them comfortable, I want a full set of neurological observations on them' Alice demanded.

The staff obliged.

The clearing up took most of the rest of the shift and by the time the day shift came in to take over, all was as normal as possible, considering the events of that night.

Alice's shift however was far from over; she had called the I.C.U. staff on duty that night into her office prior to leaving the hospital. She was a little pissed off and heads would roll.

Johnny and Dawn were joined by Barrie and the student. They had recovered and bowed their heads in shame as they entered the boss's office.

'So, who is going to start telling me what the hell happened last night?' it was a rhetorical question as she did not allow Johnny to start his story, he shut up.

'Are you aware of what your antics caused last night? How many people were frightened, hurt and overworked, staff, patients, everyone because you decided to mess about with the occult... this cannot and will not happen ever again, am I clear?' she paused.

Johnny recounted what had happened in some detail; they had made a Ouija board and thought it would be funny to try it out as per instructions on the internet.

'I, well we, are really sorry for what happened, I had no idea that this would happen'.

Alice shot off her chair and angrily stopped him in mid-sentence 'You had no idea that playing with a bloody Ouija board, in a hospital where people die very frequently and in a hospital such as ours, with its history, are you that stupid?' she added.

'What in heaven's name possessed you to undertake this irresponsible action? Oh, before you even think of smirking, that was not a pun' continued the fuming senior nurse.

Johnny did not answer and he joined his colleagues in silence.

Surely they would never do this again. They had opened the gates of hell for a mere seven minutes. Luckily

Barrie had thrown the makeshift board to the floor
when the ghosts, ghouls and spirits started to manifest
themselves managing to halt their progress.

Although most of the damage was repairable and
relatively minimal, there were still a lot of costs
incurred. There was also the small matter of the
reputation of the hospital, this was irreparable. She
emphasised the possible psychological damage to
patients and the staff members who would definitely
consider coming back on a night shift as a possible
liability. Alice made these points clear. She also
informed them they would have to pay for the damages
once assessed.

They were given a written warning, a formal step in the
disciplinary process however they were not sacked.
They were lucky to keep their jobs, their livelihoods and
were sent on their way, relatively unscathed.

The Ouija board was destroyed and therefore this key to
the gates from hell were now lost. The hope of never

having a recurrence of this was higher now but could it stop it ever happening again? Only time could tell.

That infamous night would be embedded in the local folklore, for all the wrong reasons. The stress and frightening materialization of proof of beings from another world, another dimension being able to visit our world could not be questioned. There were many who had lived through the maniacally menacing night, able to corroborate the story, able to give testimony to what they had endured and witnessed.

Warnings to all staff were issued, never play with a Ouija board, especially in a hospital. Despite the fact that Ouija is a derivation of the French and German words for yes, this was a NO-NO!

It was however not the end of it all. The hospital was blessed by a variety of different religious pastors. Christian, Jewish, Muslim and Hindu, the administrators and managers were taking no chances.

A virtual squadron of multi-faith clerics had descended on the old building. They had undertaken mass, rituals involving flowers and showering the many corridors with gallons of holy water.

The varying chants and prayers were offered and recited in all of the wards within. It was a religious union that had collaborated to battle against evil.

With all the incantations and flurry of activity,  it was hoped that the haunting had been halted, never to be experienced again...

As for the three perpetrators, they had fallen in the esteem of their peers. Time would be a healer but not for this trio.

Barrie met his demise two months later to the day. He was about to defibrillate a patient that had suffered a cardiac arrest on his ward when the defibrillator unit short circuited and he administered 360 "killer joules" to himself.

His cardiac arrest was irreversible.

Dawn was burnt alive when having a sneaky cigarette before starting her shift, four months after that fateful night. The smouldering ash that had dropped in her pocket combusted and she was found burnt to a crisp outside the hospital. Again it was too late to do anything to save her.

Johnny lived for six months before he lost his life on the I.C.U. He had become entangled in a long length of oxygen tubing and as he panicked to free himself, fell over onto a trolley that had been prepped to perform a chest drain insertion and stuck the tube inserting metal trocar through his neck, dissecting both his jugular vein and cervical spine, killing him instantly.

Although the hospital had been blessed and cleared of any ghosts, it seems that in the end it was not all clear. The unusual and unfortunate end of the three perpetrators of the Ouija board cast an uncomfortable eye on the hospital from the health and safety services.

However their deaths were never linked to any spectral interventions.  Not obviously...

It was rumoured that supernatural Justice had been swiftly and efficiently served?

## The Children of the Grave

St Augustus hospital had been an old workhouse in the days gone by, expanding its residents during the industrial revolution. It was a long time before health and safety and children's acts were developed and enforced to protect children. Young people were used as part of the labour force and their immaturity and inability to fight the adults made them susceptible to injury, mutilation and even death.

Although there was an acute paediatric ward in the hospital, the numerous sightings of children in the hospital were not of the current in-patients but the populace of the past.

These rascals were blamed for many of the annoyance s and nuisances that continually occurred in the hospital, day or night in the original part of the building.

Call bells came on in empty rooms, blinds in patients windows went up and down on their own, things went missing, especially toys and shiny items, like a bunch of ghostly magpies, they took them and made their way with them. They disappeared and many were never to be found again.

Another favourite trick of these ghoulish children was to switch channels on televisions, usually at the essential plot points. It was as if they were following the

programmes themselves and then disrupting the
viewing to achieve maximum effect.

 As if this was not troublesome enough, there were
giggles heard that seemed to originate from beyond the
grave.

The laughter was usually comprised of more than one
voice, as a deathly choir had congregated and the
disembodied crowd were laughing at the tom foolery
and chaos they were creating.

Judging by the pitch and tone of the cacophony of
voices, they were very young, once. Pre-pubescent and
therefore taken too young. They were generally an
irritant or a pest but they were not malevolent spirits.

This was until the figure of a young child was making
itself visible to the patients, young and old as well as
staff and visitors.

The figure would be seen standing in doorways at any
time of the day or night but the dark hours were when

this figure could be seen more clearly.  There was no specific doorway that the apparition favoured; it was far from selective but only in ward 5. Although spooky and uncomfortable, nothing ever happened; the manifestation would appear and just stay there as if planning its move but never taking any next moves.  It was hard to judge the sex or age of the child from beyond the grave. The definition was not sharp enough to allow further definition. All that could be identified was that it was thin, young and human. The soft glow it radiated blurred any definition.

One night though it all changed soon after a young patient had been admitted. Rosie was admitted following a barbiturate overdose that had been swallowed with the aid of a large volume of alcohol. The 19 year old had taken this fatal cocktail with the intention of committing suicide.  She had tried to end her own life as she had had enough of fighting the anorexia nervosa she had battled with for so long. Thankfully a passer-by stumbled upon her lifeless body in time to alert the emergency crew who had assisted her and prevented another meaningless end of another young life.

She had a tube passed in A&E that allowed her stomach to be washed out and activated charcoal to be administered once the fluids run clear to absorb any drugs left within the now empty stomach and prevent absorption of the drugs.

Her lips and face were black, no not due to the effects of the medication but because of the spluttering she had done as the stomach pump was removed, spilling some of the charcoal onto her face and clothing. Rosie was now connected to a cardiac monitor that was showing sinus rhythm and no effects from the overdose. Her blood pressure and other vital signs were stable and she was now responsive to some stimulus. She was therefore transferred to the ward for observation, ward 5 had a free bed and that was where she went. She would spend the night being monitored and observed and referred to the psychiatrist in the morning.

The ward staff made Rosie comfortable once they transferred her onto a bed from the uncomfortable A&E trolley with a mattress that was as comfortable as trying to sleep on a gammon steak. The admission paperwork was completed and her observations were checked with a view to monitoring them every 30 minutes. The cardiac monitor was attached onto her chest via the three leads, a red, a green and a black lead and the machine began to beep as it displayed her beating heart maintain life.

Rosie was fast asleep, her pupil reactions were getting slicker and she seemed to be on the road to recovery.

It was now 3am and Nurse Watson, who was allocated to look after Rosie, among other, made her way to undertake her routine check on the young patient.

As she headed towards room 3, the room where the young O.D. patient had been admitted to, she got distracted. Another patient had called for a bedpan, desperate to empty her bladder. Her delay was only a matter of a few minutes, when she heard Rosie's cardiac monitor alarming crazily. Things seemed to be far from okay now as she raced to the room where the alarm bells were originating from.  She entered the room which was extremely cold and uncomfortable; she could sense evil and then focused. She was now looking at a dark figure of a child; well it looked like a child. It was kneeling on the young patient's chest with its hands firmly placed over the patient's nose and mouth. Rosie, still groggy from the barbiturate cocktail, was not struggling. The monitor indicated that her heart was racing, tachycardic from the stress she was now enduring and there was no respiratory effort being made, how could there with a demonic obstruction on her chest and airways.

The apparition now looked back at the attending nurse and hissed at her in a feline like style as if warning the worried nurse away. The dead eyes on the ghostly materialization were glaring and fixed on her, its mouth open enough to bare a set of teeth that although were not solid, she was not going to take a chance on. Nurse Watson just screamed at the top of her voice. She then picked up a clipboard that was resting at the bottom of the patient's bed and threw it at the wicked shape in front of her.

Her aim was good and although the figure was not solid, the flying clipboard dislodged it from the patient but not far enough to be completely safe as it crouched creepily at the bedside, now focused completely on the brave nurse that was standing at the doorway, shaking and trembling with fear but still attentive enough to save Rosie.

Thelma and Kitty, Poppy Watson's colleagues run in to the ward in response to her scream.

'God almighty, what is going on girl, you're going to wake everyone up?' Kitty asked.

'That thing, look' Poppy said as she pointed at the evil diminutive demon that had just tried to kill one of their patients.

Both nurses screamed in fright which in turn made Poppy shriek!

'Jesus Christ, what the fuck is it?' Thelma asked with urgency as she forgot all semblance of professional etiquette.

'I don't know what it is but we have to get rid of the little evil bastard' Poppy answered.

The spirit was still there and not frightened by all the attention or the efforts to shoo it away.

At this point, Kitty, the quieter and more pious of the three spoke directly at the spirit.

'Please leave Rosie alone, she has done you no harm. She needs our help and you cannot be here anymore, move along please, your time here on this earth is no more'. She was not done she added more 'stop bothering her, stop hurting her and go, in the name of god almighty please leave this world and go with god, go into the light, find peace'. The last addition to the sentence brought goose pimples to the listening pair 'Please remember you have died'.

With those words, the evil seemed to dissipate from the evil child's face. It now looked like a boy, a sad and lost child that appeared sorry for his actions. He now simply vanished, no creepy pops or smoke screens, the apparition was now no more. The temperature in the room started to return to normal. The cardiac monitor started to show sinus rhythm and Rosie took a big breath of air, replenishing her lungs that had been absent of life giving oxygen. She was alive.

Rosie suddenly opened her eyes and asked 'where am I, am I dead?'

'No dear, you are very much alive and with luck and judgement, you will remain so for a very long time'

Thelma replied as she smiled and tucked her in the bed that now had a life on it as opposed to a corpse.

The nurses were now reassured she was safe. They charted her vital signs and moved out of the side room and headed to the ward kitchen to get some coffee and a sit down.

Poppy now had to translate the ghostly high jinks into some kind of sensible and comprehensible report. She sat at the desk in the office and worked on the report.

At handover that morning, the charge nurse was given a summary of the events of that night. He was taken aback by it all and proceeded to tell the tired and weary night shift about "Jimmy".

They had known about Jimmy for a long while but he had never behaved like this before.

'I wonder what the catalyst was?' Andy asked rhetorically. Then he recalled that Jimmy, or James Lee, had died in the old workhouse from malnutrition. He had died in what was now room 3, in ward 5. His spirit had tried to attack patients with eating disorders in the past but never to this degree of harm. He further recalled that 17 years previously, when Andy was a student, had been the last reported attack.

He asked 'How are we going to prevent any further episodes? '

'Well Kitty performed a sort of exorcism last night so that may be the last we see of Jimmy' said Thelma abruptly.

'He did appear to be in peace soon after this so it may well have worked' added Poppy

'We hope his spirit is at peace however in order to maintain safety, we must never admit anyone with anorexia or a diagnosis similar to it, into this room, ever again' Andy stated with assertion.

They all agreed that it may be a short term solution but it was safe.

However, Jimmy never re-appeared. He never darkened the doorways of the ward and no one was ever hurt.

This did not stop the rest of the little rug rats who continued to haunt the ward and carried on with their silly games and annoyances. No one was in danger and no one was hurt so their mischief was tolerated.

After all, it could be worse and they had experienced it?

## <u>The Hanging Woods</u>

During its incarnation as a lunatic asylum in the early 1930's, the grounds at St Augustus hospital were closed. The tall fences and natural borders were developed for two reasons, to keep the inquisitive public out, but more importantly, to keep the inmates in!

The inpatients were subjected to experimental procedures that were barbaric and painful.

ECT, Electroconvulsive Therapy, although still used today, was less refined. It involved a massive amount of electrical volts introduced into the patient's brain in order to "shock them out of their insanity", insulin comas were also induced as well as aversion therapies that were conducted on many, including homosexuals with devastatingly detrimental effects, some resulting in deaths. Sleep treatments and coma inducements were also inflicted indiscriminately on this populous. In an age before pharmaceutical products were developed to control psychosis, straight- jackets were commonly used as was the practice of restraint for the more troubled individuals.

The patient population ranged in differing diagnoses and levels of danger. Some were judged to have been a menace to society and 'criminally insane'. They were held in this reserve of insanity by both the structures and the staff that were employed for their menacing size and ability to contain trouble. The army of orderlies kept a watchful eye on their patients and were not adverse to levels of cruelty that are deplorable in today's healthcare systems. Pain and punishment, although not prescribed, was condoned as necessary. It is no surprise that many of these inmates repeatedly attempted to escape, few were successful, for many, escape came in the form of suicide.

Battling their troubled mental states and the conditions they were housed in was too much for many of them and if the opportunity arose to commit suicide, they took it if the experiments with electricity, new medications and other barbaric acts did not kill them first.

Hanging by the neck on makeshift ropes, bed clothes and belts, especially from the many tall trees that were cultivated in the grounds was a particular favourite.

Patients were allowed to roam the enclosed expansive grounds and many were unsupervised as escape was easier said than done. During its 28 years as a psychiatric unit, there were eighty four patients deaths recorded as suicides. An astounding fifty two managed to take their own lives through hanging. Forty two of them did so in the woods in the luscious grounds of the asylum.

Having suffered such pain, anguish and violent deaths, it was little wonder that the grounds were thought to be haunted. There had been several sightings of phantasms in the woods, ghostly figures that would hang off the branches of trees and other stories decades after the hospital had become an ethical institution.

Many of these apparitions were seen during the day by visitors to the hospital.

It was on a crisp spring day that a small car entered the ground of the vast building. It was 2pm and the car was occupied by a young family from out of town.

They had driven in and stopped inside the grounds.

Their directions to a bank had been wrong as this structure clearly wasn't a bank.

'Bloody sat-nav' the adult male, the dad, exclaimed in frustration, 'it's a piece of shit and that bloody policeman clearly couldn't direct a fart out of a colander' he continued as he bashed the steering wheel in frustration. The young family were lost, they were tired and they were trying to drive through this town on their way to their destination with an urgent need for some respite.

The two young children were also quite impatient. Aged 6 and 8 years, they needed a toilet break and a walkabout. The family were getting cranky and mum, although trying to keep calm addressed her husband and firmly said 'Derek, it's no good using that language in front of the boys, stop and ask someone for directions, like I asked you previously, please'.

Derek, with a sigh answered ' yes dear' before muttering 'I asked the fucking policeman and this is where it got us' in a low voice.

Evidently not quietly enough as Martha huffed and said 'do not take that stance with me'.

Derek turned his engine off and let the family out of the hot and stuffy vehicle for some air and respite.

The boys, desperate to urinate, run out of the car, pulling their trousers down, found a corner behind a tree and peed until their bladders were comfortably empty.

Martha and Derek examined the map, re-calibrated the sat –nav and hoped they could get a good GPS signal but alas, it was not working.

'Piece of crap your father bought for us, it's useless' the annoyed man exclaimed.

Martha just gave him "that look" and he soon looked down at his feet and shut up.

There was no one around as the shift change and hand over was at 2 pm, not a soul to be seen. Also, they had come in through an alternative entrance to the grounds, not the main entrance and therefore less likely to see others.

'Boys, please do not meander too far' Martha called out to the boys who by now had finished their call of nature and were picking up leaves and sticks.

Derek hatched a plan, 'I am going to go in that building and find someone and ask for directions to the bank, okay?'

'Great idea, Martha' replied with a definite air of sarcasm and he headed off to the big edifice that was not far from where he had parked.

Derek soon disappeared into the building and Martha remained by the car, listening out to the two young lads who had a bit of freedom to play for a while without being confined to the car and the imprisoning seatbelts that tied them down.

It was a good fifteen minutes and Martha sat quietly, listening to the birds singing in the trees, hearing the laughter of Tony and Jimmy playing. She was enjoying the scenery with its towering green trees, the feel of a refreshing wind on her face as she sat in the car with the doors opened. She was so comfortable; she drifted off into a light sleep after all they had been on the road for ten hours and she had remained awake throughout this time. Martha suddenly woke up with a start. It was too quiet, she could still hear the tunes of the birdsong but she could not hear her children.

'Boys, boys, where are you?' she called out. There was no reply. She called again and this time, she could hear the boys calling out with a panic in their voices. She could clearly hear Jimmy, the eldest calling out 'Mummy, help us please, we don't like this and we don't like them'.

Martha sprung out of the open car and run towards the direction of the source of the voices. She run and called out 'its okay boys, mummy is coming'.

She darted towards the boys and she could hear them sniffling and crying.

They were only around fifty yards away but it felt like a mile as the young mum, heart in mouth, dashed to the rescue of her offspring.

She was soon at their side and she grabbed both children in a protective grasp however they were transfixed on something. They were both looking up at the tall oak tree, their little faces were ashen and their eyes fixed firmly upwards as they held on to their rescuer, their mother.

'It's okay boys, I am here, you are safe' Martha reassured them, however they clung on and remained icily fixed on something that was above them. Martha turned and directed her gaze towards where they were looking.

She yelled and grabbed her children, hugging them and pulling their heads away as she detected what had frightened them. Just above her, there were two people hanging from the branch that jutted out from the trunk of this almighty tree. Like a pair of creepy Christmas decorations, they bodies swayed from the tree, appearing lifeless yet their eyes followed the troubled trio below.

Both bodies were male and they wore what seemed to be straight-jackets as their arms were not visible. The whiteness of the cloth was blending into the pasty look of the ghastly faces and their blood red eyes were fixed on the children and mum. It was at this point that the body on the left shrieked madly, bringing goose pimples to the frightened mum. Her hairs were standing on end, as if on high alert. The next lynched body then started to laugh, an evil cackle as they hung there on the branch.

Martha cried out 'fuck this' and grabbed the boys, lifted them up with some supernatural strength that she had suddenly found and run. She run and did not look back. At this time, she could clearly hear more voices, mad laughter, eerie cackles and groans coming from other trees but she run quicker.

Her target was in sight, the family car, a lump of tired red metal was her goal. The safety of the car would protect them, especially if she could drive it away from the woods, nearer the building and shelter.

She threw the children in, instructing them to do their belts up and then run into the driver's side, reaching for the key when she realised, Derek had taken the keys with him.

'Derek you dumb fuck' Martha muttered in disappointment.

She looked up and saw a multitude of bodies in gowns and straight- jackets climbing off the trees, like a troop of demented apes... she was scared.

In a panic, sweating, breathless and disturbed by all of this, she was just getting ready to run again when she saw Derek walking toward s the car in the near distance.

He was distracted with his face firmly examining a piece of paper in his hand. These were obviously directions to the bank but he was oblivious to what was happening.

'Derek' Martha screamed and he looked up.

He now saw his distressed family and the imminent danger ahead. He ran towards the vehicle, covering the distance in seconds. He clambered into the car, keys in hand and turned the ignition. With a roar, the diesel engine kicked in and he put the car in gear, put his foot down firmly on the accelerator pedal as he let the clutch go and they were off with a screech of rubber. As they drove towards the spine-chilling forms that approached them, they all screamed as they drove through them covering their faces with their arms in order to protect their faces when they crashed. However the anticipation of a wallop or collision was never realised, they drove through what simply could have been just a memory or an apparition. Derek looked into the rear view mirror and all that was visible was the dust cloud from their speeding vehicle. No bodies, no chasers, nothing else but dust.

'What the hell were they?' Derek asked.

'I have no idea, just keep driving' was Martha's response...

Either way, they did not seek any explanations and sped out of the grounds of St Augustus, even out of town. The bank could wait; they would try their luck in another town...!

## <u>The Nun of Death</u>

No self-respecting compilation of ghost stories would be
complete without a creepy nun story. There is
something about their dark habits, uniform as opposed
to their inclinations. Their legs unseen under the heavy
dresses, they seem to float effortlessly over any terrain

that can freak people out. It is ironic that these peace loving and helpful members of the Catholic Church can somehow terrorise people with their attire...!

St Augustus hospital was no exception to the apparition of a veiled form or two. It had not only been a convent at one point in its relatively long life but also Nuns had long been nurses too.

Reports had been numerous about the nun that could be seen at the old staircase that led from the care of the elderly ward on the ground floor to the male medical ward. Ward 11 was a particular favourite site to meet "Sister Fatality" or "The Nun of Death" as she was more commonly known.

This grand, winding staircase flowed up the side of the huge hospital wall, its gigantic wooden steps were adorned by heavy gilded banisters and ornate iron spindles. It was a beautiful architectural feature in the daylight however at night, it transformed into a disturbing stairway from hell. Its shadows formed from the dim light bounced off the hard surfaces around it forming unearthly and bloodcurdling forms to make the bravest of people fearful. It was not helped by the repulsive gargoyles that also accentuated the baroque style stairwell.

As if by pure bad luck, the stairs were also leading to the mortuary corridor.

It was in this vicinity that a figure of a nun had been seen silently ascending, and not climbing, the noisy wooden stairs. She had been seen by many and the pattern of apparition seemed to coincide with the death of a younger patient. She would be seen floating up from the area of the mortuary and she would disappear into thin air at the top of the stairs.

As the hospital grew, the extensions off it were fabricated in different styles, in keeping with the style of the era and the quirkiness of the architects. Ward 11 had been styled as an old "nightingale ward". A large room that housed twenty eight beds with half the number of beds arranged on each side of the ward with screens that could be drawn around the bed if privacy was needed. It also had two side rooms which were used for the dying patients or patients who needed to be isolated due to infections. These were popularly renamed as the "departure lounges" because of the links with the dying patients. They were situated in a long corridor at the beginning of the ward and faced the stairs. There were also another two rooms off this corridor, a linen room and a small ward kitchen. The kitchen was the last room on this corridor and was the first room one would see when visiting ward 11.

As part of the night shifts duties, a nurse would fill the oversized hot water urn at 5 a.m. in order to provide the patients with a nice warm pre-breakfast beverage when the lights turned on again at 6 a.m. with the accompanying drugs round.

Joe Ellis was an experienced staff nurse on the ward who was used to the rigmaroles of shift work. He had

worked in hospitals for all his adult life and had heard
many a story including stories of the phantom Nun at St.
Augustus Hospital; however he had personally never
seen her, well not yet anyway... the mysterious cloaked
woman that would appear on the grand staircase had
eluded him.

The twelve hour shift was near its end, it had been
unusually busy with four overnight admissions, one of
which resulted in the demise of one of the newly
admitted patients. The death, however distressing it
was to have a death in any shift, coldly meant more
paperwork, emotional work in the dealing of grieving
relatives and less time to rest.

This gentleman who had sadly passed away had been
suffering with severe emphysema and was in the end
stages of his disease. He had contracted yet another
chest infection and was admitted for treatment of his
exacerbation with intravenous antibiotics, steroids and
high doses of bronchodilator drugs. However, despite

the best efforts of doctors and nurses attending to him, he had coughed and spluttered, gasped for air in distress until the morphine he was also given to alleviate his shortness of breath had kicked in. He was now at peace and no longer suffering; he had now shuffled off this mortal coil, and at eighty seven years of age had peacefully passed away.

His family had been with him until the very end and they had time to hold hands, speak and bid their farewells. Percy had moved on with dignity. His family had now left the ward; the deceased received his last offices and had now been transferred to "Rose Cottage" code for the mortuary.

Joe had updated the copious notes along with his colleagues who had shared this hectic turn of duty.

Although he was a much respected member of staff, Joe was hiding a secret. He was a two timing womaniser. He had bedded many of the less scrupulous night staff during the years and was now involved in a long and torrid love affair with one of the nurses on the same shift as him who worked on one of the neighbouring wards. He and Christine would sneak out and meet, covertly, in any available nook or cranny and continue their mutual lust and infidelity, unpunished. They had been very discreet and remained undetected but the events of the night had meant they had been unable to congregate and consummate their bodily needs. Joe was a little anxious to meet his "bit on the side" but tonight, this would be unfulfilled.

He had just finished his hot cup of tea and got up off his chair with a big stretch and yawn jokingly saying 'I suppose I'd better fill the urn up seeing as none of you lazy lot will do it'.

Dinah, one of the other nurses replied in an equally jovial manner 'It's about time you did something you lethargic sod'.

They laughed and he made his way out of the office and headed toward the kitchen at the end of the corridor.

He hoped he could at least snatch a moment with Christine. Maybe run to the ward where she worked in, plan and encourage a dirty liaison on the next shift?

'Brrr, it's always bloody cold here' Joe muttered to himself as he felt the sudden drop in temperature. He continued none the less, thinking 'the patients would be quite upset if they didn't get their early morning tea'. However he was also anticipating robbing a surreptitious snog and fondle of his lover.

He had now reached the kitchen and started to fill the oversized urn with numerous litres of water from a jug, a process that would take a good few minutes. As this continued, he started to prepare the trolley to convey the beverages when something caught his eye. It was strange because it was not in his conscious field of vision but appeared to be behind him, as if a feeling that he could see. It compelled him to turn around. As he turned, he momentarily caught a fleeting glimpse of an ill-defined dark figure on the stairs. It was a quick flash because it was no longer there. In a blink of an eyelid, the figure had gone. Although only less than a second's worth of sight, he could define the dark, blurred vision enough to know that this tall, cloaked figure dressed in black from head to toe definitely resembled a nun.

'Nah, I'm just tired' he said to himself, 'there isn't anything or anyone there' as he tried to reassure himself and turned towards the kitchen and concentrated on the task at hand.

With the urn now full to maximum capacity, he switched it on and then picked up a packet of biscuits to hand out with the early morning tea or coffee. As he did this he had turned to face the kitchen door again and jolted in shock as he faced the apparition again, with the grand staircase in the near distance. He was now face to face with this tall dark figure he had seen only brief moments before. This time he was able to set some detail to it; her face was far from friendly. Piercing white eyes on the darkest backdrop imaginable were

119

staring straight at him, relentless and unmovable. They were dead soulless eyes.

Joe could immediately feel a cold sweat pour from within him accompanied by a crushing central chest pain, like a large vice being tightened on his thorax, preventing a purposeful breath, expelling the life giving air from his lungs. He was now feeling drowsy with the hypoxic state he was quickly suffering from, and then it all went blank.

He awoke seconds later, or so he thought. He was now surrounded by a plethora of nursing and medical staff. He tried to get up but he couldn't, he was unable to move, Joe had no energy to lift a limb and the headache he was experiencing was a thousand times worse than any other he had ever had before.

He now attempted to get off the floor only to find that he wasn't on the floor but on an uncomfortable hospital bed. He was hooked up to a multitude of intravenous infusions and monitors that beeped away in the background. He was connected to the heart monitor via three electrodes firmly attached to his chest that coupled him to this machine via the lead, like a long umbilical cord connecting the unborn embryo to its mother's womb and just as fragile.

The din from the concoction of voices, electronic beeps and buzzes together with whatever medications were now freely running through his veins only worsened his confusion. Slowly though, his fuzzy head became more focused, some clarity was returning, he could now decipher the voices; it was the hubbub of healthcare professionals in conversations seeped in jargon. 'EEG this, ECG that, SVT, M.I., rhythm strips and ectopic beats'...

'Hang on' he thought 'I think I must have had a heart attack?' He needed answers; he was frightened and desperate to get to the truth but as much as Joe made any attempts at conversation, the Endo-tracheal tube that was firmly and very uncomfortably sitting in his mouth, reaching into his windpipe, was stopping any articulation or communication. He was at the mercy of his colleagues.

He now reminisced on the set of circumstances that had brought him here to this point of despair. He now remembered meeting the nun of death. As he did, his cardiac monitor picked up an abnormal rhythm and alarmed.  He suddenly felt the bed head drop and he was now flat on his back as the nurses rallied around him and started to compress his chest. He felt the pressure surge in his chest with each and every life giving compression. The pain intensified as he became more aware of the facts that lay before him, he was acutely aware of his own mortality and impending death. Joe was also aware of the cardiac monitor beeping crazily away in a rhythm less cacophony of electrical noise. The monitor was now showing ventricular fibrillation, an irregular, pulse-less action that was as unproductive as a non-beating heart in asystole.

'V.F. arrest' was now being loudly muttered among the attendants. More drugs were being pumped into his veins; he could feel the cold sting of the chemicals entering his body in an attempt to rectify the situation.

The pain became more intensive.

It was just before the darkness took over again that Joe saw her again, the nun of death was in the room with him, her evil presence getting closer, her deep and dead eyes claiming his full attention, he was getting colder as the room got darker and then the last thing he heard was a constant and monotone" beeeeeeeeeeeep"...

## <u>The Mural</u>

In 1914, the orphanage had recently re-invented itself. Commissioned as a hospital, at this point was still very much an orphanage. It was still a hopeless and bleak building, despite its more positive transformation and function.

St Augustus had been through several changes already and in order to revitalise the building, a benefactor, a rich industrialist that had moved into the town during the heady days of rapid business growth and Victorian low scruples, donated a large sum of money to bring the building back to life with some colour and light.

The hospital director, Mr. Samuel Stephenson, had approached Albert Howard, an up and coming young artist who was quickly getting quite famous, very sought after due to his attention to detail, vision and composition. His reason for contacting the young man was the fact that someone had died who had left a considerable amount of money in their will to improve the children's ward. Creating a colourful and friendly mural was one of the stipulated conditions of the will. He was obliged to comply to this.

Stephenson was an accountant and not versed in environmental psychology. He was not really interested in an environment that promoted security, hospitality, care and wellbeing.

To him, the books needed to add up and that was his priority. 'We must remain in the black and not in the red' was his motto and mantra.

Albert's father had been one of the many children of the old workhouse and had told him many a horrific story of living and working as a child in the condition he and many of his contemporaries had endured in their early years. He had vivid memories of the dark and depressing surroundings, cold and inhospitable buildings of the Victorian era. He longed for some happiness as a child and commented on how just having some colour secreted in some areas could have made some difference to the perceptions and horrific experiences they had suffered.

Albert was determined to make a difference and since he now resided in the town adjacent to St Augustus, he had offered his artistic prowess to brighten up the children's ward in the hospital.

He had met with Mr. Stephenson who had agreed to have this relatively famous artist to paint one of the clinical and bare walls of his hospital.

Albert was commissioned to create a scene that would both distract and assist the young patients in their recovery. Through the colour, composition and care, Albert Howard would help the needy paediatric patients and somehow help heal the ghosts of his father's past. It was unfortunately too late for Mr Howard senior to appreciate his efforts to address his past, tuberculosis had consumed him and he had sadly passed away in one of the hospital wards only months previously. None the less, this would be a fitting homage to his memory.

Albert had been summoned to the director's office, a vacuous administrative centre with an over exaggerated oak desk that occupied a large space within the chamber. The room smelt musty and although the windows were large, the heavy red curtains that were adorning them prevented the life giving light from penetrating the room. Large oak bookcases adorned the expansive walls that contained medical books bound in heavy leather casings as well as other medical curios that decked out the shelves.

Albert thought to himself, 'this man seems a little pretentious and as a Mr. was he a surgeon or just a failed doctor?'

He sat across from the director on a chair that was half the size of his hosts. This was obviously another statement of power.

'So Mr Howard, have you got some sketches to show me so I can take them to the board?' Mr. Stephenson ordered coldly and quite commandingly. Although he had agreed to accept the artists work to be permanently displayed on a large mural, his intentions were only to gain publicity and the extra injection of cash, not through care or compassion.

This meeting felt more like a formal interview than a chance to give some joy to the infirm. Albert however was not going to react to the discomfort he felt and would continue with his intentions and goal.

'Yes of course, I have them here with me' the young painter replied.

In a gruff voice, Stephenson remarked 'Please let me have a look at them; we need to vet them before you go ahead and start to change the décor of our clinical areas with any old adornments'.

Albert handed over his preliminary sketches and ideas to the grumpy director, Stephenson placed his monocle over his left eye and leered at the drawings letting out an occasional 'humph' as he pondered on them.

He turned toward the young man and addressed him in the same "superior tone" he had commenced the conversation with 'I suppose they will do, I will speak to the board tomorrow at our meeting and will let you know our decision tomorrow at precisely 3:30, do not be late, good day to you sir' he said as he stood up to shake the young artists hand and dismiss him from the meeting.

Albert now eyed the man in all his stature, powerful but quite tiny!

He shook his hand and silently vacated the office through the gigantic wooden doors and headed off down the corridor toward the exit. It was at this point that his mind seemed to go into overdrive and he made a decision to visit the children's ward.

He made his way there with a purposeful stride, tipping his hat and smiling at staff members as he directed himself to the ward.

He had finally got to the children's ward, the only ward in the hospital with a name rather than a number. It was named after the main protagonist of Daniel Defoe's fictional work of the 1700's "Robinson Crusoe".

'Robinson Crusoe Ward is a strange choice considering he was shipwrecked and marooned on an island, it conjures up feelings of loneliness and solitude' the young artist thought. 'Then again Defoe's tale does have connotations of adventure and hope... maybe it is appropriate to this environment?'

He opened the door and found numerous children on beds that although tidy and functional looked quite uncomfortable. The surroundings were dreary and clinical, far from a happy place. The children were gloomy; they looked sad, miserable and fed up, strangest of all, they were not playing, they were inactive.

There was a very obvious and distinct lack of happiness, toys, colour or joy. He definitely needed to celebrate life in his work, an injection of colour with the provision of hope and healing.

Albert introduced himself to a young Staff Nurse, informing her of his purpose, asking if he could look at the ward and find the best place to paint his masterpiece on.

'Please carry on' she replied, following this with a firm 'please do not disturb or talk to any of the patients'.

An injection of humanity and humour was urgently needed and he would make it a personal crusade to address the needs of the "children" and not "patients" that occupied the beds.

He had examined the architecture and finally found the ideal place for the work of art. The large bare plaster wall that faced the main entrance to the ward, it would be visible by any and all who entered the area, visitors and staff alike.

The painting would evoke a sense of joy and wellbeing with the hope and impetuous need to help the young sick and infirm who temporarily reside past the point of access, creating a doorway of optimism.

The perfect spot would portray the ethos of the ward which would ultimately be, "to cure the sick" but with some joy and care to boot...

He left the bleak building and made his way home with hope in his heart, a plan to return the subsequent day and attain permission to commence his joyous masterpiece.

It was now 3:15, Albert marched down the now familiar corridors towards Stephenson's office. He was not intending to be late and awaited the decision of the board. He soon reached his destination and sat on a small chair outside the big doors awaiting the answer to his painting. He felt like he had returned to infant school, sat outside the principal's office awaiting some corporal punishment for a misdemeanour.

If it was a "Yes" he would devote the next few weeks to creating a masterpiece that would challenge the surroundings and achieve a corner of happiness. If the board decided against his proposal, well there was no challenge that could be met but it would be so unfair on the young patients who would inhabit the ward in the future. It would be a defeat to mankind, caring and hope.

Albert looked at his shiny pocket watch attached to his waistcoat. The clock face marked time accurately, it was 3:29. The point of no return was imminent.

As if driven by Obsessive Compulsive Disorder (O.C.D), the doors opened at exactly 3:30. Stephenson's secretary walked through them; she looked over her glasses and addressed him.

'Please follow me' she stated. A cold morsel modelled in the same mould as her boss, she demanded he follow her into the office where the verdict of the meeting would be instructed to him.

Albert followed her into the musty office and was now at her boss's side as he continued to look down at the papers that were meticulously set on his large desk in front of him. He did not acknowledge him for a minute or so and once he had heavily signed the paper, he addressed his gaze at the young artist.

'Ah Mr Howard, the board have agreed to commission your art for the children's ward, so can you please sign this waver of responsibility should you screw things up?

He continued to talk at him rather than to him: 'This essentially frees me, or should I say our establishment from any legal responsibility should you create a monstrosity and the repercussions are to be targeted at you only'.

Albert paused to think for a second and then replied 'what the hell, what's the worst that could happen?

He signed the legal document and thanked the insipid Stephenson and left the room with a big smile of victory on his face. Before he left, he turned to the director and asked about start times and dates; Stephenson just looked up at him and said, 'Miss White, my personal assistant will give you the minutia of the details, good day'.

Albert was tempted to call him something disrespectful but opted to think it instead, 'What a prick!'

136

The cold administrative sidekick presented the young artist with the itinerary and as he looked at it, agreed to start as stipulated, a week from that day.

He made his way out through the same route he had exited the previous day, near automatic pilot, however this time, he would not visit his soon to be work area.

He now had to concentrate on the paints: the base colours, the bright colours and character depictions that would enhance the immediate environs of the ward and create a happy place. It wouldn't take much to change the mood of the area but he wanted it to be a statement piece, homage to his deceased dad and a masterpiece by any other name.

He had estimated the work would take three weeks and in order to comply with his meticulous and fastidious employers, he had to remain within the deadline.

The next week had arrived and Albert had been busy purchasing all the paints, brushes, pencils, ladders and cleaning fluids to commence his undertaking.

He had left everything in a cupboard on the ward, under lock and key. He was now ready to start his project.

The area to be painted was cleaned and the plaster on this wall, chosen to display the mural was smoothed, cleaned and made ready on day one. He had occasional glimpses from the children that snuck out to see the stranger, the visitor who was busily playing with one of the walls.

Albert soon painted the base colour, a vibrant mix of blues and greens that would sustain the rest of his artwork onto it.

The scene was quickly coming to life as he pencilled in the characters, some were imaginary and some were modelled on a few of his visiting admirers, the children themselves. They laughed at the drawings they clearly recognised as themselves. The work was not finished but yet they were already laughing, a sound that had been alien to this building!

The days went by, turning into weeks when soon the work was nearly finished. It was a country scene full of happiness and characters that seemed to come to life. The colours were vibrant, successfully bringing the best of the outside world into the unhappiest of buildings.

The project had taken a little longer than the planned time as he had made many friends whilst painting the mural. He had spent time teaching some of his young visitors how to draw, paint and laugh. This took time and he was not going to complete his commission in time.

There were still a few finishing touches to be added but the masterpiece was going to remain incomplete. War in Europe, the Great War needed men to fight it.

Albert, like many of his friends and neighbours decided to serve in the local regiment. These regiments were springing up in towns and cities all over the country.

It was a sad last day when he left, his admiring patients and some of the nurses felt they may never see him again. Albert's response, he painted himself in the mural, he was one of the gondoliers on the river that flowed through the mural.

'Please don't worry, I will return and complete this, however I will never be gone as my spirit will always remain with you in the form of my portrait'. It was deeply philosophical but heartfelt.

Albert went off to war, never to return to the hospital. He died on one of the skirmishes in one of the fronts in France, a victim of a mustard gas attack that killed him on the battle field.

The news reached the hospital and even Stephenson shed a tear.

The mural was never finished, it was truly a homage to life and happiness, his father would have been proud of his efforts.

Albert's pledge to never leave was truly realised as the gondolier, Albert's depiction of himself could be found in a different area of the mural every day. Like a mystical 'Where's Wally', children would search the mural for the painter and find him smiling back at them.

Through this inexplicable evolution of his art and his spirit, through his sacrifice, he not only attained hope in an otherwise grey building, he provided mystery, intrigue and fame. This in turn, allowed "Robinson Crusoe Ward" to remain in the limelight, thus protecting its users, the children and families from being mistreated.

Their guardian angel would look after them for eternity.

Now this may sound sweet and not scary at all, however when the ghoulish gondolier is not sighted, that is when people have to worry.

In his mission to protect the vulnerable children from harm, any person who was harming, abusing or not caring for their children would feel the wrath of Albert's vengeance. His victims certainly knew when they had met his spirit...

*I'd like to take this opportunity to share this book with my wife, Julie.*

*She agreed to co-author this book and as a fellow nurse who has experienced the wards and shared stories with other colleagues, the following are her welcome contributions.*

*I am sure you will relish this chilling story as have I.*

# DEVILISH DUTY

## CHAPTER ONE

It was a scorcher of a heat wave, enthusiastic Elizabeth Perrill had divided loyalties commencing her stint of night duty, after spending four glorious days off having quality time with her family. She was particularly proud of herself for having faced the criticism of the elders in the community, when she had married, started a family and decided to study nursing, all before she had reached her 20th birthday.

Although wanting to be accepted as a mature woman, Elizabeth still wanted her childhood nickname Bessie. Bessie rollicked in being a rebel. The only time she shot to attention when her full name was used, was when her mother scolded her, or Matron Lotte Peigne or Night Sister Angelica Strutt reprimanded her.

It had been an extremely stressful period in her life, although Bessie tackled any challenge like a terrier with a bone.  Bessie was determined to show the world how she could utilise the energy of her tender age, to juggle motherhood and a career to ensure she reached her life goals.

In order to keep up with her mammoth list of "daily things to do", Bessie had adapted herself to a military style procedure of home life, studies and work tasks. Her single peers would have spent the first day of returning to duty, having chilled at home relaxing, sleeping, and possibly boozing at the hospital social club.  Bessie's life was a world away from her fellow student nurses.

She felt vocated to nursing. Her auntie had nursed as a nun, she was so proud of Bessie, she gave her a tiny silver crucifix necklace.  Auntie Mariam had placed the necklace around Bessie's neck, advising her it had been blessed by the Bishop of the Diocese.  It would ward off evil spirits; therefore Bessie was never to remove it.

Bessie was not superstitious, but respected her Aunt's request and love for her.

Bessie had not been allocated to any particular ward, therefore had to report to the night sister for instructions. The day had dragged on longer than usual. Bessie was feeling drained having to force herself to walk tall in true nursing etiquette, as taught by Sister Strutt.

Bessie's mind was distracted, full of words, images and questions as she rushed down the stone corridor. The heat was intense and her head felt it would explode from her stressors. The glimmering trees seeped a trickle of strange blinding light through the corridor windows. The shadow shapes dancing in the long corridor made her feel an eerie presence.

Abruptly, Bessie was thrown across the corridor from a flash of lightning and thunder clap simultaneously bursting through the corridor's dainty gothic window. A perfect storm had commenced.

Bessie clambered upright, collecting her scissors, pens and cap that had been strewn across the gleaming floor.

'Full moon you know, it'll only get worse' complained a late visitor scurrying towards the exit.

'Charming' thought Bessie as she patted down her uniform.

She checked her fob watch for damage and was mindful of the time it would take her to get to Sister Strutt's office. Bessie advanced her pace to a trot.

On arriving at the Night Sister's office, the door was ajar. Sister Strutt was at her desk engrossed in paperwork under the over-sized desk lamp. Bessie stood erect whilst gently knocking her knuckles on the freshly painted door. Sister Strutt peered sternly over her reading spectacles.

'You're late nurse Perrill' scorned Strutt

'You'll never guess what happened to me in the corridor Sister' Bessie bantered.

'I don't wish to hear your excuses young lady.  Patients are relying on you to care for them … on time.

Especially today, we have an unusually high number of staff absent.  I have not seconded you to a ward, as you will be covering staff breaks throughout the hospital.  Here's a list of wards and times for you to report.'

She handed Bessie a list in the most exquisite handwriting.

Bessie had not yet mastered the art of hiding her emotions, her face sunk into melancholy.

'You can wipe that expression off of your face nurse.  You are here to motivate, educate and nurture very sick people.  Practice smiling even when you feel as if you will cry.  The future of healthcare depends on you' instructed the very experienced Sister Angelica Strutt.

Bessie's mind played back Sister's words to the image of Lord Kitchener's First World War poster, pointing his finger at Bessie saying

'Your country needs you'

Bessie grinned as she lost attention of the conversation, and started fiddling with her crucifix necklace. Sister Strutt squawked at Bessie,

'You know the dress code nurse Perrill. No jewellery. I insist you remove that at once and I will have to write a report, as this is not the first time I have .......'

Suddenly the desk rattled as the clanging telephone bell evoked the telephone to samba dance across Sister's paperwork.

'Sister Angelica Strutt speaking, how may I help?'

'Are any other patients involved?'

'Where is he now?'

'Okay, I shall go straight to Casualty'

Sister Strutt slammed the telephone earpiece onto the receiver; her concerned face looked up at Bessie. Sister flapped her hands ushering Bessie out of the office.

'Saved by the bell' Bessie whispered gratefully and
rearranged her uniform collar over her necklace.

## DEVILISH DUTY

## CHAPTER TWO

On arriving at Ward Pio, the senior nurses from the previous shift and all the nurses from night shift squeezed themselves into the Sister's Office for the shift handover.

Gloria (nicknamed Glo) nudged Bessie with her saggy chubby elbow, flapping her upper arm's excess skin, across Bessie's wrist in the process.

Glo whispered 'Ere, Bess. Ya know why no one's turned up for work don't ya. It's only a full moon innit'.

'I knew it, 'cause I've got one of my flippin' headaches and Casualty was bursting when I walked passed, from my locker'.

Glo was a middle aged Enrolled Nurse, who had worked on the ward since her teens. She was a reliable knowledgeable nurse, never missing a shift come rain or shine and was a natural leader. Glo had long ago decided not to further her training to staff nurse level, sacrificing her career for her family commitments.

Glo added 'Oh, and you'll never guess what happened to ...'

Staff Nurse Dora Ball scowled 'Gloria, we will discuss that later when we have more details to share, meanwhile, let's get on with handover to release our day colleagues'.

Bessie's senior, Staff Nurse Dorothy Babbage, was her assigned mentor, unfortunately also the bane of Bessie's life. Bessie believed that there was nothing she could do right in Dorothy's view. Dorothy had the knack of enabling Bessie to feel totally inadequate and subsequently a nervous wreck. Any mistake Bessie had incurred, Dorothy had witnessed and reported back to Matron and the night sister. This caused many a bad atmosphere at shift handover meetings and task allocations. It also had caused Bessie to work more independently of her supervisor, for fear of being ridiculed or criticised in front of the patients and student peers.

Bessie wasted no time, collating her list of things to do with her assigned patients and raced down the ward with the comfort trolley.  This trolley was equipped with all that was required to attend to patient's pressure areas and settle them for the night, or until the next round every 2 hours.

Bessie was already starving hungry.  Her rumbling stomach was embarrassing her, especially during the intimate silence of taking the patient's pulse and respirations.  The ward was not full; however the whole hospital being short staffed, resulted in duties being stretched throughout the staff that was available.

The last patients to check on her rounds before Bessie would leave for the next ward on Sister's list were in Side Ward A.  Four sturdy antiquated white metal beds created the impression of children's cots arranged around the out of date room. One bed lay empty and was not quite as white as the other three, in the shadows.  It had what appeared to be an iodine or burn mark on the metalwork.  These were old beds from the original sanatorium.

In three beds lay elderly female patients who were sound asleep, snug as bugs in rugs.  Their teeth all grinning from the watery depths of the standard issue gleaming glass tumblers, on the polished wooden bedside lockers.  The bed tables were neatly sat at the bottom of each bed, decorated with ornate glass vases housing aromatic lilies.

The orchestra of grannies were snoring in sympathetic harmony, each in varied tones of nasal whistle or snort, accompanied by the crescendo of wind instruments (farting), ranging from lady-like squeaks backed by the let-rip kettle drums, all conducted in unison to the forte of the ever reliable antique clock's tick, with its' bold

Roman numerals peering sternly from high up on the wall.

Opposite the clock hung a huge wooden cross, an abandoned remnant of the building's origins. Proudly centred on the high ceiling hummed the dependable yet obsolete fan. This mesmerising windmill in the sky diffused the rooms' bowel, blood and urine niff, metamorphosing into a fusion of the lily's sweet bouquet mixed with Olde English Lavender talcum powder.

The wind howled round the building like an angry banshee and the rain pummelled the fragile glass windows of the ward. The bright moon shone across the ward floor like the opening scene of a Hollywood movie, she half expected Fred Astaire and Ginger Rogers to gracefully tap their way across the satiny polished boards.

Leaning over bed A1, she was observing Mrs Chamber's shallow respirations when, all at once, she heard the nurse call buzzer emanating from another side ward.

Rushing out to check, she carefully crept through the large swing doors, so as not to wake the peaceful, flannel nightie brigade.  As Pavlov had famously conditioned dogs to salivate on hearing a meal bell, student nurses are conditioned to instantly react to the nurse call buzzer, by immediate investigation and risk or priority assessing (maybe not salivate), per contra practice their personal bladder control pelvic floor exercises, as they miss yet another break.

Scanning along the corridor walls for the identified flashing light, she jerked slightly in a double take.  For there in front of her glowing like a lighthouse bulb twinkling in the mist, was indeed Side Ward A light flashing above the door she had just tiptoed through.  In her perturbed mind she reasoned

'This was wrong surely, the old dears were all stoned from the chemical cosh of tranquilisers, sedatives and analgesia (pain killers), and nobody was awake…. I think'

In a shudder like a dog drying from a shower, she had instantly become cold. She fiddled with her uniform, as it had felt like the hairs on her back had stood to attention and re-aligned her outfit in the process.

She wished she had been more self-disciplined by shaving her neglected hairy legs, instead of taking that extra five minutes snooze this afternoon.  Now they itched irritatingly across the mountainous goose bump terrain.  The crucifix was jingling from her rapid breathing, making her even more conscious of her jitters.

Tiny torch held firmly in her trembling hand, she crept towards side Ward A doors.  Glancing through the chequered safety glass door view window, she could only see her own tired reflection in the glare of the sparkling pane.

This triggered a muffled gasp 'Argh'

She had not recognised her own reflection of her cap skew whiff on her now spikey hair.

Trying to avoid contaminating her hand, she twitched her nose with a silent sniff shuffle, which was about to dribble clear salty mucous. Her hands began to tremble and her teeth chatter. She contemplated,

'Blimey I really do need a cuppa and toast. Tea-break is calling me. I'm cold, confused and probably more hypo (hypoglycaemic) than the chaotic diabetic patients. I could have sworn that buzzer was from another side ward, the corridor night lights seem dimmer now and why has the temperature plummeted to a wintery chill?'

Diligently, she raised her arm to open the big old door in clean practice technique with her elbow.

As she shuffled silently into the side ward, immediately she was aware that the cubicle climate had sunk from comfortable ambient room temperature to a bleak icebox.

As she stepped into the room, the door slipped from her arm closing itself with a loud click.  These oiled doors were usually silent without a lock mechanism.  She turned her head sharply back to glance curiously at the door handles.  In the dim light there appeared to be a locked metal bolt across the door.

'Where the hell did that appear from?' she scrutinized.

Reaching out to grab the bolt, her arm was dragged back to her side, by what felt like a magnetic force. She stood frozen, not from cold but fright.

A sudden cackling yell provoked her to swerve round to face the ward again. To her amazement, there was now a patient in bed A4.  Bessie let out a muffled squeal midst jumping out of her skin in horror.  She gawkily fumbled her way back to beside the door in the dark.

Promptly visually scouring the room for a head-count, she was not disturbed that there were now four patients in the room.  This was a rare, but not surprising occurrence in wards, when wandering confused or disorientated patients returned from the toilets to a different bed.

Bessie felt uneasy tiptoeing over to bed A4 preparing herself for the chaos of waking a nervous patient whom was oblivious of playing musical beds.  In despair of this situation, her mind was digressing.  By being in A4, the wanderer had clinically contaminated the vacant bed. Bessie would now have to change the sheets on this bed in preparation for an emergency admission.  For as long as Bessie could remember, Night Sister Angelica Strutt considered Bessie to be bother.  Bessie sighed to herself

'This delay will be another step down my career ladder'.

Distracted with her thoughts of work, Bessie had not realised that the other patients were now silent, no snores, no wind chimes, yet they were not stirred by the shrieks of the patient in A4. It was as if the room were frozen in time, misty and blurred.

Bessie's back was rigid.  She stopped in her tracks and could move no further.  She felt glued to the spot as if something or "someone" was keeping her from moving, almost guarding the area from her trespassing.

The patient was mumbling a weird language Bessie had never encountered.  Although the room was now below freezing, with windows rattling, there was heat emitting from bed A4, rising into the air in a cloud of steam.  The patient had covered herself with the top sheet like an Egyptian mummy, crumpling the starched linen.

'Calm down dear, I think you are a bit lost, come with me and we'll find your own bed' Bessie stammered.

The unknown person in the bed pulled down the sheet to reveal herself. Glowing in a haze of orange, she stared straight at Bessie.

'Whose eyes are those staring back at me? Did I imagine this?' she blinked and cautiously opened her eyes.

Suddenly, there again were the evil bright amber eyes penetrating Bessie's soul. Unrecognisable as human eyes, Bessie tried to fathom what she was seeing, by repeatedly blinking to refocus and make sense of the appearance.

'Is it evil?'

Bessie could only translate the person's eyes as goat or sheep like.  In the dark room, they blazed from the person's micro cephalic head directly towards Bessie. She could feel her heart palpating in her neck and a crushing holocaust in her heart.

The being bellowed at Bessie in an incomprehensive jabber

'Whoa, ccccc, shiayyyy, zghodz'

Bessie replied 'Ppppardon dear?'

The freak now angered at Bessie, hollered

'En a senbay oh op vayd fall'

Then rotated its' head away towards the wooden cross high up on the wall, squirming as if in excruciating pain, at that instant abruptly swinging her strange face towards petrified Bessie.

'I will kill you'

Bessie bounced backwards losing her balance, her legs still frozen rigid, she gulped to halt her gut about to eject bile.  Her face was burning with the heat from the hideous squatter, her throbbing eyes stung.

In an unprofessional moment of panic, abandoning the three dormant matriarchs, Bessie turned on her heels and ran for the door.  As if in slow motion, her body became heavier, as she neared the exit. Her steps shifted to exaggerated laborious astronaut moon walking pace.

'I don't wanna die' Bessie whimpered to herself

'Grab the handle, grab the flipping handle' she ordered her limbs to reach out to the door that seemed miles away.

The metal handgrip coldness electrifying shock shot through her fingers up to her elbow, like a reverse of hitting her humorous (funny bone). She flinched for a second, took a firm hold, promptly properly swinging the door open inwards into the magnetic room.

Thereupon she immediately recognised a safe warm feeling transpire throughout her body and mind. The corridor night lights performed more brightly, the whining wind had gone, her tense body slumped into relaxation. Bessie was exhausted. She swivelled prudently on the look-out for the new banshee inmate.

Dumbfounded astonishment hit Bessie. Side Ward A had three patients, in obvious comfortable slumber, their deep respirations in tandem with each other. Bessie gingerly pushed the cumbersome door ajar with her shoulder.  A waft of warm ambient lavender and lily air tickled her runny nose.

Taking a deep breath, she weakly took a fleeting look at bed A4. There in the corner was the military style perfect bed ready for the next admission.  No special effects, just plain old hospital vista.

'What on earth is happening here?' Bessie quizzed herself

Her head was dense with turmoil as she shuffled across the room to check the three convalescents slumbering contently.  Satisfied all was hunky dory, she accelerated her stagger to blast off out of the room.  Bessie glanced through the viewing window again, the room was normal, nothing untoward anymore.

A feint sound echoed down the corridor from the other end of the ward

'Nurse Perrill, stop dreaming.  Gloria's back from her break, where have you been?' Dora whispered loudly with no regard for the sleeping patients.

Bessie left them to their own devices, as Hugo the chatty old porter looked like he was dying to tell them both something.

Bessie clung onto the comfort round trolley in a giddy daze.  She could not find the words to respond to Staff Nurse Dora.

'Who on earth will believe what I just saw?' muttering along the ward Bessie questioned herself.

She glanced down at her ever reliable, ever right, never wrong fob watch.  She realised she was late for relieving the next ward team.  Bessie hurriedly placed the trolley back into the bright sluice room, sniffing in the disinfectant aroma.

She grabbed her cape and bag from the ward office and nervously greeted Dora and Gloria, and waved to Hugo,

'Ta ta for now'

As she abandoned Pio Ward, bewildered Bessie prayed to St Crescentinus (patron saint of headaches).

'Maybe the ole bat, Sister Strutt, is right; the saints might just help me through the shift'

## DEVILISH DUTY

## CHAPTER THREE

Disturbed by the spine-chilling event on Female surgical, Bessie was keen to get to her next ward to cover for staff breaks. The event had delayed her by 5 minutes and she dreaded that someone would relay this negative error to Night Sister Strutt. It was going to take a steady pace and speediness to get to the original older part of the hospital, that had windy stairs and less lifts.

As Bessie raced down the hospital corridor, her thick cape flew behind her. She caught her superman like reflection in a window and imagined herself as super-nurse flying over the ancient building, saving the hospital from horrific dangers like earthquakes or plagues of locusts.

From the running, Bessie's cap had tilted backwards in her hair and the Kirby grips had rambled around her head in all directions, her thick belt was meandering in circles forgetting where the front had been and her cape was entangled around her neck and arms.

As she neared the approach to the next ward the realisation of her duty snapped back into her brain. Bessie halted to take a breath and compose herself.  As she exhaled rapidly, she vaulted into the air with a shriek 'Arrgh'

A porter had been gliding around the corridor bend and collided with her.

'Hugo you scared the life from me'

'Ha ha ha ha!  Bessie girl you'll outlive me' Hugo sniggered as she drifted off down the corridor.

Bessie burst through the huge squeaky doors of Roch Ward.

'Cholera' Bessie shouted in her mind

'Patron saint of cholera'

Bessie always praised herself of her mind mapping memory tool for remembering the ward saints. This she practiced daily in order not to get caught out by 'religious Sister Strutt'. Bessie always got irritated with Sister Strutt's emphasis on the holiness of the building and not on the exciting innovative new medical technology immigrating into the establishment.

'You're late nurse Perrill' growled enrolled nurse Reka Goldspink

'Oh no' Bessie sighed to herself

Reka continued 'You're gonna make the whole shift off sink now Perrill, you really are a joke'

'Oh, leave her alone Reka, it's okay Bessie darling you're only a few minutes over' interjected Staff Nurse Harvey Gaye.

'We're happy to see you Bessie' nudging Reka in the arm

'Aren't we Reka?' Harvey glaring at Reka

'I suppose so' Reka sulked

Although younger, Harvey was senior in rank to Reka, but being far inexperienced and an innovative dynamic nurse, he often ruffled Reka's feathers with his new techniques and ideas unsettling her routine. Harvey revelled in reading all night about medical advances, whilst Reka appreciated the office light off for an all-night snooze on the arm chair she had shanghaied.

Reka was middle-aged and treated Harvey as a son, usually embarrassing him tidying up his uniform, flattening his hair with a motherly stroke on his head, or speaking over him during reports to night sister Strutt. Harvey took it all in his stride.

Reka was convinced Harvey was homosexual, so she believed he required extra smothering from her motherly urges. Her conclusion was because Harvey had never mentioned a girlfriend or his personal life. No matter how hard she tried to clumsily interrogate Harvey in a Socratic manner, he entertained himself relishing in teasing Reka's small mindedness and was determined to keep her guessing for as long as possible.

'Well Reka, do you want to go to first meal break?' enquired Harvey

'No' snapped Reka

'I'm going to catch up on my rest; I've been on my feet all day with my rabble at home'

'I really need a shut eye to re-charge my batteries'

'I'll go to second break after you Harvey'

Harvey suggested 'I'll take a shorter break Reka, so you won't go hungry'

'What? And lose out on sheep counting? I think not Harvey, you take your time son' instructed Reka in her matriarchal tone.

Bessie was stood in the middle of these delegating two, she felt like an eager ball boy at Wimbledon following the rally bouncing left to right. Reka continued to talk over Harvey whilst he attempted a rushed handover to Bessie. Harvey showed Bessie some journals they were mutually passionate about, eventually making his way off to the hospital canteen.

Reka noticed Bessie nervously playing with her necklace.

'Oh Bessie dear, don't let Angelica Strutt catch you with that round your neck'

Bessie told Reka about what had happened at her last near miss in Sister's office. She quizzed Reka how she had gotten away with wearing jewellery.

'Well my dear, Angelica and I were students together, back when dinosaurs roamed the land' she winked at Bessie.

'What's she going to do to stop me? Confiscate my stethoscope!' Reka contended.

They both giggled.

Reka snuggled herself in her armchair, having raided the laundry cupboard for fresh cosy blankets and pillows. Bessie scurried around piling up patients notes preparing herself for Reka's nap, when Bessie would read them under the dim desk lamp. Reka was just closing her eyes when she woke with a startle.

'Bessie, the boiler's on the blink' Reka exclaimed

'The water urn has a touch of the ole timers and is taking so very long to boil'

Reka digressed

'Oh there's something I must tell you, have you heard? Oh, I'll tell you after with tea'

'You'll have to fill it up and put it on low, so it's heated in time for waking the patient's for their 6am medicines. Thanks darling' immediately Reka closed her eyes.

Bessie shook her droopy head in dismay whispering to herself 'Some bloody super-nurse I am'

Reka had 30 years of night duty to practice on demand slumber; subsequently she was an expert at seemingly spontaneous REM sleep. Before Bessie could grumble or enquire about the ward, Reka's head was tilting forward, mouth gaping with her loose bridge dentures escaping onto her bottom lip.

'What a lip-sticky toothy grin Reka, careful you don't spook anyone' Bessie muttered

Reka now comatosed was beginning to snore and her collection of gold jewellery was glistening in the twilight.

Bessie left the office as quietly as she could, with a quick peek at dreaming patients lined up along the blacked out ward. She giggled, bemused by the involuntary noises filling the sick bay.

'Definitely different to Pio Ward, patron saint of stress' Bessie knew off by heart in parrot fashion.

Roch ward was male surgical and had not been modernised to 4 bed units. During the transformation from institution to hospital, refurbishment funding had been overspent. Therefore, Roch and a few other wards remained in their grand original Florence Nightingale fashion, like a long dance hall.

Hence, the plethora of sounds echoed from the mostly healthy working aged men with fractures and post-operative minor surgery. Unlike the grannies of Pio, the men's farts were smellier and noisier, their snores were like lighthouse foghorns and unfortunately flowers were rarely available in male wards, consequently the mix of body odours was not masked.

Bessie knew any nurse calls would go straight to the office where Reka was resting. For this reason, she had no concern leaving the large ward, to attend to the kitchen outside Roch main door. These were creaky parts of the vintage super structure, as a result Bessie was accustomed to the groans of the building, especially on a night like this with winds attacking the gothic flimsy window panes and yodelling along the cold limestone corridors.

Health and safety was not a priority when the hospital was converted, thus there were no doors between the kitchen and the corridor. The only equipment in the kitchen of danger and worth stealing was the refrigerator and water urn, along with a trusty tea trolley. The quaint wooden cupboards housed plain crockery and utensils for patients use, along with a few personal cups and glasses staff had brought in from home. It was a boring white clinical room. Bessie was not looking forward to wasting her precious time filling up the towering water urn using the miniscule jug provided.

Opposite the kitchen was a grandiose iron veranda imposing over a palatial, open, dimly lit stairway, glistening with flickering dying night lights. The magnificent moon beamed through the stained glass window, glistening colourful ballroom butterflies across the atrium. Bessie daydreamed (although night-time) staring out to the ornate veranda entranced from the shimmers, whilst performing her factory assembly line style of urn filling.

She imagined her Hollywood dancing idols Fred sliding down the bannister and Ginger tapping gracefully, trustfully folding her body into his loving arms. Bessie's mind wandered off to her ambitions of travelling the world. She wished she had been able to sit and read Harvey's impressive medical advancement journals, to empower her hungry mind, instead of playing Aquarius in this cell.

Without warning, above the howling wind, a thud and squeak resonated from the stairwell. Bessie's startled ears pricked up.

She immediately spotted a hunched dark figure disguised in a cloak, wheezing and grouching up the flight. In a flash, the strange physique confidently elevated to eye-level with terror-stricken Bessie. Her heart aflutter she was sweating bullets. The bogeyman's bony paw grabbed the oak polished hand rail at the top of the stairwell, slowly groaning as its' structure snapped during erecting itself to final ascension.

Still clutching the water jug, Bessie squirmed in the door way, weak-kneed, face to face with the gargoyle. With eyes tight shut and lumpy throat, Bessie snivelled

'Reka, h-e-l-p'

The creature wobbled backwards gnarling at Bessie 'Oi Oi Bessie girl'

Bemuddled Bessie prized open her eye-lids, simultaneously the visitor tore off its' dark cloak to reveal itself.

'For the love of God, Hugo, you scared the life out of me again' Bessie uttered huskily

There, stood in front of her, was chuckling Hugo Dodkin, a porter whom Bessie guessed to be as old as the

182

building.  Hugo was a short, skinny, wheezy chain smoker.  His bones crunched as he cheerily slogged his shifts around the hospital.

Bessie pushed Hugo in a jokey manner on his arm

'I didn't recognise you with that cloak on'

Hugo shook the wet over-garment.

'I've just taken a body to the morgue Bessie, God rest his soul what a cruel night to meet your maker.  Full-moon.  It's chucking it down out there in the courtyard, the rain is un-relentless.  So I borrowed a cape someone had left in the mortician's room'

Hugo chortled deafeningly 'Ha ha ha ha, you should see your face Bessie girl.  You look like Sister Strutt had caught you wearing that necklace, ha ha ha ha.  Never you mind her, just keep wearing it my girl'

Bessie wondered to herself about ward Pio strange events, trying to rationalise how she may have imagined the whole process.  Musing, she carried on her Aquarian role of filling the water urn, as she watched Hugo's bent shuffling silhouette disappearing along the vast corridor back to the main hospital.

Bessie chuckled to herself

'Gosh I am a bag of nerves tonight, my imagination is prolific, maybe I'm dehydrated, it's been so hot today'

She paused from tip-toeing filling the huge urn, to rummage through the cupboards searching for a glass for a cool drink of water, to counter balance her over-active thinking machine.

Kneeling on the numbingly cool floor tiles, Bessie reached into a deep cupboard to grab the sole tall glass waiting for her at the back.  She sat back onto her heels, in a trance from staring into the sparkling vessel. She rested for a second before manoeuvring herself to stand.  From the corner of her eye she saw a shadow beyond the veranda on the murky stairwell.

'Back again Hugo' she laughed blindly, as she rose to her feet in the bright kitchen.

There was no response.

'Is your hearing fading Hugo?' She shouted jokingly

Tentatively she listened. Alas still there was no reply. Bessie curiously walked out of the kitchen, clutching the empty glass in one hand and leaning on the veranda with the other. She fearlessly rubbernecked over the rail.

Bessie froze to the spot, blinking in an attempt to re-focus on Hugo running down the stairs. She concluded it was not Hugo.

Instantaneously her sweaty palm lost grip of the glass, in a flash it shattered across the landing floor, bouncing fragments like confetti on her chilled legs. Bessie did not flinch. Her heart raced. She could only feel her fob watch tapping on her bosom and necklace dancing on her heaving chest.

There was no walking sounds from the old warn steps. There was no clunking, creaking or thumping. A short, petite female shaped figure silently floated from the landing downwards. She was draped in a long hooded black loose cloak, with her hands clasped in front. From her praying hands dangled incandescent rosary beads. Her head gazing at her holy mitt, the muted, apparently pious, spectre hovered slowly gravitating. She descended reaching the bottom corner newel post, instantaneously disappearing.

Still hanging her head over the veranda, Bessie remained gawping at the empty stairwell. A waft of incense crammed her tiny nostrils. She shook her head frantically snorting out the strong cloudy aroma.

All at once there appeared flickers of what seemed like cobwebs floating in front of her face. Stamping her way backwards on the broken glass, Bessie tottered like a zombie into the kitchen.

'Could it be that the ghost is warning me of danger?'
Bessie questioned

She gazed out of the window in confusion as the
scenery was replaced by a floating silent mist
approaching the building.   Bessie told herself

'Why am I scared?'

'For God's sake, pull yourself together woman, you're a
nurse!'

So she stealthily cleared the glass, trying not to damage
her gleaming leather shoes.

'Boo!'

Bessie yelped again in shock and nervously looked up
from brushing the floor.  It was Harvey grinning like a
Cheshire cat, giggling,

'Bessie chill out, you're a bag of nerves'

Harvey offered to finish off the water urn and sent Bessie off to her next ward, as she was behind schedule again.

# DEVILISH DUTY

## CHAPTER FOUR

Bessie ran up the corridor to the lifts. She was late for her next ward on Sister Strutt's list. Her ad hoc plan was to save minutes by catching the lift up to the modernised wards. Sadly, the lift call light on the wall was not moving along the numbers, which meant someone had left the door open, parked at operating theatres level.

Groaning to herself, Bessie continued the steeple chase of stairs, nimbly leaping 3 stairs at a time, to reach her destination. She was an Olympic athlete of hospital corridor sprints; hence she boasted a healthy pulse and blood pressure.

Bessie slowed to a bouncy stride as she entered St Quentin Ward.

Her signature mindful reference to patron saints was not forgotten, she whispered to herself,

'Patron saint of coughs'

Chuckling under her breath 'It would be far more appropriate with a Russian sounding saint like Benny Linforchestikov'

Smiling to herself, Bessie wandered the dark ward looking for the staff.  After meandering back up the ward, she was startled by a black shadow edging towards her from the brightly lit sluice room.

'Bessie, what are you doing creeping up on me like that? You'll give me a coronary.  We just had an admission from Casualty, poor lady suffered a CVA (stroke), I'll end up in the bed next to her' complained Ivanna.

Enrolled Nurse Ivanna Tush explained that her colleague Staff Nurse Lola Fibbs had been summoned to Casualty, as the department was bursting at the seams.

'Did you hear about what happened ...? Let me tell you. Oh, I think she's not even down in Casualty, she'll be in Private Ward flirting with the rich patients and that prat Staff Nurse Max Cockburn' Ivanna gossiped.

Ivanna went on to explain to Bessie, how she planned to ask for union backing for a pay rise request, as she alleged she was doing Staff Nurse duties on Enrolled Nurse salary.

Ivanna added,

'Whilst Lola Fibbs conducts her love life from ward to ward, sniffing out willing male nurses. She gets away with her ridiculous excuses, because Sister Strutt is her Aunt'

Bessie nodded in empathy for the frazzled nurse.

Ivanna was at collapsing point of her busy shift, she complained to Bessie how her varicosed veins where making her feel she was carrying lead weights on her legs. Bessie comforted Ivanna and suggested a summarised handover to speed up Ivanna leaving for her break.

Ivanna hurried through the patient handover as Bessie accompanied her to the ward exit.

As soon as Ivanna had slipped through the ward doors, the nurse call buzzer beckoned Bessie. Rushing, she swiftly found the correct patient Mrs Ava Chance.

Bessie was beckoned by a patient who was a local school headmistress, Mrs Lena Crossland, recovering from a nasty chest infection, due for discharge the following day and looking forward to returning to school duties. Lena had been awakened from the commotion of the stroke patient's admission and was now reading a book with the aid of her overhead night lamp. Lena pointed to Ava, gesturing to Bessie that Ava was in need of assistance.

Mrs Ava Chance was the woman who had just this evening suffered a stroke. Hence she would be extremely weak and needy. Bessie encouraged Ava by suggesting things she may have asked for and showed her how to use a mixture of signs and verbal communication. It was clear Ava desperately needed to pass urine. Bessie praised and congratulated Ava for regaining her bladder control and being able to communicate her needs to Bessie.

Then Bessie stood back to think. Ava was an obese woman. How without a colleague, was she going to get Ava onto a bedpan? Bessie recalled training and ward experience techniques she had learned to roll patients onto bedpans. However, the stroke had paralysed Ava on one side of her body. This rolling technique was not going to work.

Bessie appealed to Ava if she was able to wait until Bessie could find a colleague from another ward to help manoeuvre Ava onto a bedpan. Ava looked dismayed. As Bessie listed the options in her head, Ava began to cry in pain and embarrassment.

Bessie held back her own tears at seeing this patient so helpless. Bessie was tired, dehydrated and still on tender hooks from shocks she had endured at the previous 2 wards. She dashed to the sluice room to locate a warm bedpan for Ava.

Bessie returned to Ava within seconds. As Bessie dragged the privacy curtains to a close, Lena whispered audibly to Bessie,

'I didn't know we had male nurses on this ward'

Bessie was puzzled at Lena's statement, but far too occupied to bother continuing the conversation, with that she grinned at Lena and closed the curtain around Ava's bed.

Bessie hurriedly explained to Ava that on the count of 3, with her good leg and arm she was to push upwards, whilst Bessie would lift Ava's affected side from her bottom area.  Bessie slipped one arm under Ava's buttocks.  She asked Ava to concentrate hard and pray that both of them will find the strength as a team to get Ava on the pan.

Bessie counted to 3.  She managed to lift one side of Ava.  Poor Ava was unable to move herself.

Bessie looked up to the ceiling, took a deep breath and begged,

'Please God help Mrs Chance'

Suddenly, the privacy curtain ruffled as if someone walked through the gap.  Without hesitation, Bessie felt Ava become weightless as she lifted Ava up as high as Bessie's shoulders and lowered her slowly onto the warm bedpan.  Bessie and Ava's eye's met then both of them looked at the curtain.  A trickling sound of passing urine into the metal pan relieved Bessie's mind and Ava's fragile body.

'Let's roll you off of the pan gently now Mrs Chance. Gosh you must be more comfortable now that's done'

Ava pointed to the curtain, and then lifted her hand up into the air, looking muddled.  Bessie felt heat spreading from her wobbling legs up into her stomach, then a sudden stifled feeling.  Then something brushed passed her legs, leaving a chill down her spine, causing her to shudder.

'Yes, Mrs Chance, I really don't know my own strength. It must be the tasty spinach pie I had for my lunch'

Bessie settled Ava to as pain free position as possible, then opened the privacy curtain.  By surprise, Lena whispered loudly, as teachers do so professionally,

'Could you check my sputum pot please, I think I need another'

Bessie responded to Lena 'I will be with you in a short time Mrs Crossland; I have to go to the sluice room first'

Lena's face altered in an unimpressed stance.

'Not you dear, the young male nurse who has just been helping you with that lady behind the curtains'

'Hey, nurse can't you hear me?'

'Look at him walking off ignoring me'

'What's his name?'

'Can you ask him please, nurse'

Bessie presumed Lena had been talking to her, but she had seen and described a young male nurse going into, coming out of the privacy curtains and walk off down the corridor.  Bessie had seen no-one.

Bessie's hair raised, on the back on her neck for the umpteenth time that night.  However, she did not feel fear, only bewilderment and awe for the support she had received from this guardian.  In the sluice room, Bessie caught her reflection in the huge window; her crucifix necklace was glistening like an orb.

# DEVILISH DUTY

## CHAPTER FIVE

At the end of the lengthy shift, Bessie shuffled down to the depths of the hospital to the locker room.  There chattered a room full of nurses changing into their uniforms for the day shift, like a hierarchy of angels preparing to spread good will to the sick and dying.

Glo and Reka were standing by their lockers, with their arms crossed, pushing up their cleavages as they exchanged updates to each other.

Bessie nodded to each person she squeezed passed, until she reached her own locker.  She was too tired to converse and carried on with changing her clothes like a robot.  Bessie listened to the banter as she tried to remove her whiffy tights, peppered with rips from the glass she had dropped.

Glo sympathised with Reka,

'Oh it's so awful about poor ole Hugo, such a cheery chap he was'

Bessie woke from her automated state.

'Glo what's happened to Hugo?'

Glo and Reka both stared at Bessie and replied in unison 'He died at the beginning of our shift last night'

Bessie's legs wobbled as she sank onto the bench.

Reka stroked Bessie's hair 'Oh my darling, we've all gotta go some time. You know he was chancing death anyway smoking like a chimney. He was a good age'

Bessie stuttered 'That's not the shock Reka. I saw Hugo during the night'

'You must be imagining it Bessie, you were very tired and it was a hell of a night with that storm' added Glo supportingly

They explained to Bessie that at the start of the shift, Hugo had been called to remove a patient from bed A4 in Pio Ward.  The patient had been admitted that afternoon, after being found delirious next to a bonfire in a forest.  Nobody had understood the patient who appeared to speak in tongues.

As Hugo had been transferring the patient onto the mortuary trolley, lightning had struck through the window onto the bed.  The electric bolt had burnt the freshly dead body.  Hugo ran out from the side ward into the corridor screaming, apparently claiming the patient was an animal.  Hugo suffered a massive heart attack collapsing on the corridor floor beside the door of side ward A.

'We had to call Sister Strutt to help at Casualty.  Bessie, that was just before you arrived at Pio.  Surely you knew' interjected Glo.

Reka supplemented,

'That bed always has problems you know.  Since the days of the sanatorium, they say that a devil worshiping witch was diagnosed as mentally ill and given ECT (electro convulsive therapy) in that bed.  She cursed the ward'

'They say you are only saved when wearing a holy relic. Good job no-one's seen her in years, because Strutt has banned neck jewellery.  Do you think that's what's been Hugo's downfall?'

She continued,

'This is strange though my dears, because every time a staff member dies, the little nun in her black robes, appears on the lower stairwell praying with her rosary beads, en route to the mortuary to safeguard the dead'

Bessie gulped.

Glo joined in the myth, recalling how the wards had changed over the years, confirming that Quentin Ward had originally been a male ward.  There had been a horrific motorbike crash one evening involving a fatality. She remembered working in Casualty that night, when colleague Staff Nurse Noah Askew was the dead motorcyclist.

'Yes, and that kind male nurse Noah still helps out on Quentin ward every time a colleague dies'

The two nurses continued their post mortem of theories of how no-one had seen the apparitions last night. They revelled in dissecting the endless stories and myths from the hospital's dark past.

Bessie, slammed her locker shut, faintly waved her hand farewell to her colleagues and walked out of the hospital in a daze. Thinking to herself, as she watched the flickering light through the street lined trees,

'Remember my training; Freud clearly explained that ghosts are a mere psychological delusion'.

'Of course these were not real, I was tired. But that doesn't explain the fact that this interacted with my actions'

As she waited at the bus stop, Sister Angelica Strutt pulled up in her flash car. Bessie's hopes rose as she pondered whether Strutt actually had compassion and was going to offer her a lift. Sister Strutt wound down the crystal clear driver's window,

'Nurse Perrill I hear from your mentor Staff Nurse Dorothy Babbage, you have been joining in discussions about ghosts and such like. This hospital is not haunted. That's ridiculous; this building is a place for people to recover, where even religious representatives visit daily! Well that is just nonsense scaremongering. I certainly do not believe in that rubbish. Things that go bump in the night are just buildings creaking and light changes in the room'

'Nurse Perrill, you are going to have to pray morning noon and night to St Jude, for indeed you are a lost cause'

*Finally dear reader, please reassure yourself that nowadays we know that holograms are explicable phantoms.  Or are they?*

*J.F.Gulrajani*

Don't be a stranger and interact via social media...

Website:

http://rockape65.wix.com/author-ram-gulrajani

In keeping with the times, I have a Facebook page which is:

https://www.facebook.com/Ramsbooks?ref=bookmarks

Follow me on Twitter: @Author_man_ram

Blog: http://legallylucky.blogspot.co.uk

**Other Books by Ram Gulrajani available in ebook or Paperback:**

- **Legally Lucky**
- **Phobic Wars**
- **Mental Dental (Murder by Proxy)**

**Also see Ram's author page:**

http://www.amazon.co.uk/Ram-Gulrajani/e/B005O7JDBG/

Have fun and enjoy these stories and remember to share your reviews.

Printed in Great Britain
by Amazon.co.uk, Ltd.,
Marston Gate.